The Brightest Firefly

A Collection of Short Works

Dacia M Arnold

MOM, AUTHOR, SUPERWOMAN

Dacia M Arnold
13611 E 104th Ave
Unit 800 PMB 15
Commerce City, CO 80022

© 2019 Dacia M Arnold
https://daciamarnold.com/

All rights reserved, including the right to reproduce this book or portions thereof in any form whatsoever. For more information email dacia@daciamarnold.com or visit http://daciamarnold.com/contact/

ISBN: 978-1-7325870-5-2 (paperback)
ISBN: 978-1-7325870-4-5 (ebook)

To my little sister, Kyria. It's pronounced Keer-uh not Care-uh and since I'm older I am the authority on this matter. You inspire me every single day. I love you beyond words.

Table of Contents

Introduction	vii
Fiction	1
In An Artist's Studio	3
Sunday School Crossing	9
I Should Not	15
A Mirror Negative	21
A Love Denied	27
Dirty Bombs	33
Etched	45
A Foot Off The Ground	51
The Executioner	53
The Last Piece	61
Nonfiction	65
Writing a World	67
Little Mary Magdalene	71
Baghdad ER	75
War and Coffee	81
Life On The Extra Board	85
Mom-Clique	89
Poetry	93
Showcase	95
Masterpiece	97
Don't You Know	99
Plays	101
Is The Mind Not Of The Body?	103
The Community	109
Sneak Peak of Apparent Power:	
Book 1 of the DiaZem Trilogy	115
Acknowledgments	129
About the Author	131

Introduction

Dear Reader,

When I started writing in 2015, I knew I would see my story through to the end. December 6, 2017, my thirty-third birthday, I signed my first ever full length project to a small publishing house. Astonishingly, the book was not the only work I finished within those two years.

About three months into developing my story, and halfway through Apparent Power, I drafted myself into a hole. A major plot point wedged me into a place I could not write myself out of with a considerable amount left to tell. Instead of quitting, I took a yearlong respite from the novel and started my degree in English. I also created a blog where I plunged into new writing styles, often nonfiction. Both pursuits set me up on a journey with many roads.

This publication contains musings of many sorts and dabblings I created over the past four years. I have compiled stories here just as a child collects fireflies. They revealed themselves, rising from my imagination like tiny lights from blades of grass in the dark, and I captured them on the page, a glass jar, to share

INTRODUCTION

with you. Various sizes and shapes, each illuminating a corner of my mind to you, the reader. Though some corners may be darker than others, I anticipate you will discover one that radiates brighter than the rest.

Enjoy.

Dacia M Arnold

Fiction

Being best and otherwise strictly known for my fiction, it seems fitting to start a collection with short stories. I warn you again; I attempt nearly every genre of writing without the anticipation of failing. There are happy stories, heartbreaking and devastating ones, ambiguous sci-fi, historical, horror, romance, and a good pulpy assassin story.

In studying the craft of writing, I discovered many literary techniques. I strive daily to become a well-rounded writer and practice as many techniques as I can grasp. Short fiction is a great platform to experiment. You will find many genres, perspectives and voices emerge as I worked to find my own.

There is a sense of instant gratification in writing short stories in a sitting or two. Success in this form takes the talent of a good storyteller. You will soon discover whether I am such a writer, and hopefully to your delight.

In An Artist's Studio

Historical fiction carries a fairly intuitive explanation. With a robust following, the genre will never fade in popularity. Transportation to a distant time and place has always fueled my affection for reading. Composing this work was no exception. This story is my speculation of how the great poet Christina Rossetti discovered the inspiration for her famous poem, "In An Artist's Studio."

Ms. Christina Rossetti removed her gloves as she entered the studio of the renowned painter. She heard of his marvelous work from her charity ball, in which he generously donated paintings depicting women of all behaviors. She auctioned for her charity and traveled days to thank the gentleman in person for his kindness. But when she stepped into the dusty loft, she faced a troubling realization.

"Pardon me," Rossetti addressed a younger woman cleaning paint brushes in a back corner of the open room.

"Me, madam?" the girl appeared not to look Rossetti in the eyes but kept her head bowed in case she was not the subject of conversation.

"You. This is you in these paintings, is it not?" Rossetti motioned to the dozens of canvases hanging on the walls. Navigating through the forest of easels, Christina closed the distance between her and the working woman.

"Oh, madam, I am the assistant here. You should query the artist about his work, not me." The girl turned back to her labor but led the way with searching hands as if the room they stood was pitch black.

"My dear woman, are you inflicted?" Rossetti maintained an objective tone as to not offend the woman with her pity.

"Only just, madam. I promise you I am a competent assistant." She continued working.

"Without a doubt."

It was not her blindness that pulled her heartstring. The irony laid in every single beautiful composition in the room holding a woman as its subject. Though each in its variance of time and place, the face, and the eyes especially, were all the same. The same woman who blindly tended to the studio chores. This irony moved Rossetti so considerably that she knew she must express the beauty and admiration, evident in the artist's work to this capable woman.

Then, Rossetti mused, *would the woman's enlightenment remove all romance from the scene? The paintings she cared for, are that of her likeness; an image she may have never seen herself.*

The tragedy, Rossetti thought to herself, *is in and of itself a work of art. If I raise the veil of mystery for this woman, would her admirer lose his attraction? I shall not rob a man of his muse, but I cannot simply keep this a secret. His exploitation of this woman through his works, while she is none the wiser, is not a crime. But how high of a god does this artist feel in placing her in every conceivable fantasy he has?*

As Rossetti passed each painting, she sifted through mixed emotions on the matter. Her duty, as a fellow woman as well as a poet, to express such metaphors as man's unapologetic puppet mastery of women grappled with the beauty of her plight. While the canvases were as exquisite as the ones donated for her charity, their subject was unconsciously a prisoner.

"Can I help you find something in particular?" a man's voice snapped through her concerns.

"What is all this?" she asked before considering with whom she spoke.

"Well, if you've made it this far through the showroom and up the stairs to my studio, one can assume these are paintings. Now if you don't mind, Miss...?"

"Rossetti. Christina Rossetti. My apologies. I've traveled days to thank you in person for your contribution."

"Miss Rossetti," he emphasized the Miss, "pardon my presumption, but your inquisition betrays your appreciation. Have you discovered something disapproving?"

"Perhaps. May we speak alone?" she requested, motioning subtly toward the feminine muse who still kept busy with the brushes.

"Mary, can you see to the showroom floor? The wind has created quite a nest of leaves in the corners."

"Yes." And she went.

Rossetti, only then, regretted her request. It was not decent for a woman to be alone with a man, but she swallowed her uneasiness and began.

"She does not know. Does she?"

"I am afraid I do not follow," the artist seemed to grow annoyed.

"She is the subject of your art. All of your paintings are of her. No matter the setting, obvious only to someone who has been here and seen her in the flesh. I admittedly did not recognize in the three pieces sent on your behalf as they held markedly differing scenes. But now I realize who she is."

"Well, what leaves you in such an unsettled state, Miss Rossetti? If my donations earned their weight in the auction and in turn provided their purpose to you? Why do you have such an apprehension to my muse?"

"Keeping secrets is a form of lying, would you agree? So she works for you day in and day out, unknowingly lending herself to your intrusive imagination." At the word intrusive, Rossetti pointed out a bare-breasted whore in a tavern, seated on a man's lap. "It would occur to me and maybe others with this inclination, that you watch this woman in her most vulnerable state. Spying on her."

As she spoke, she referred to another sketch of the same woman undressing behind a screen; however, her body exposed by a strategically placed mirror that no other woman would dare position in such an angle knowingly revealing herself to anyone on the other side. The thought sickened her stomach.

"Do you, at the very least, appreciate her? If she does not know, and you wish to keep it this way, do you have a care for her as a person?"

The man stood shifting his weight from one foot to another, liking to that of a child confronted by a Sister of an infraction during mass. He walked to an easel bearing a canvas in mid-work. In this painting, the woman wore a regal dress with her shoulders exposed and her belly swollen with child. After touching a brush to it once or twice, he put it down.

"She is my twin, born minutes after me and without her sight. Our mother died in childbirth and our father when we were fifteen. I have taken care of her since we were just children." The artist paused for a moment before starting again. "I understand how this may appear, but please know, Miss Rossetti, my sister, means more than anything and I would appreciate your discretion in this matter."

Christina Rossetti bowed and left the painter in his studio. She saw his sister on her way back through the showroom, and though her conscience fought with her, she remained silent in her exit. With her heart so disturbed, yet reverent to the sensitivity of the subject, Rossetti pulled her parchment from her bag and sat on a quiet bench.

There was a powerful conviction to give voice to her discovery in this art. In her soul, it mixed within her an injustice. Aside from the tragedy in which she had only just removed herself from, there was still something to be said of the manipulation the paintings portrayed in society. His twin was his sister in the means of blood and loyalty; however, she was not his relative in how he painted her. She was anything but a sister. And in this realization, Christina Rossetti wished the world to know how paradoxical and metaphorical the experience.

So moved by the very heart of the matter she penned:

"In An Artist's Studio" By Christina Rossetti (1856)

One face looks out from all his canvasses,
One selfsame figure sits or walks or leans;
We found her hidden just behind those screens,

That mirror gave back all her loveliness.
A queen in opal or in ruby dress,
A nameless girl in freshest summer greens,
A saint, an angel;—every canvass means
The same one meaning, neither more nor less.
He feeds upon her face by day and night,
And she with true kind eyes looks back on him
Fair as the moon and joyful as the light;
Not wan with waiting, not with sorrow dim;
Not as she is, but was when hope shone bright;
Not as she is, but as she fills his dream.

Sunday School Crossing

In 2018, the Horror Writer's Association chose to resurrect the popular children's book "Scary Stories to Tell in the Dark". I took to social media to ask women what their fears were. That was when I met Cheri. She leant me her childhood fear which mused my entry for the horror collection. While I ultimately did not make the cut, I gained a friend and an interesting perspective. Thank you, Cheri, for being vulnerable and honest.

Cherry spent all night fussing over her green dress with sunflowers on it. She cleaned her shiny white shoes at least four times. Mitchell, her fourth-grade neighbor, and best friend invited her to church. He said there was ice cream at the end of the children's service. Even if Cherry had not had a crush on him, ice cream was enough motivation to go. She woke before her alarm that Sunday despite having only a couple hours of sleep.

Cherry had been inside churches before. She attended weddings, and once a funeral service of her father's uncle, whom she had never heard of. Otherwise, her family was not the church-going type, as her mother put it. Cherry understood the concept of God but never learned the major details of religion. It did not take long for the Sunday school teacher to have Cherry's full attention.

"The devil is clever but wants nothing more than to lie, cheat, and destroy everything you hold dear. He is like a little voice that tells you to do things that might not seem naughty, but could hurt you or others."

The more the teacher spoke, the clearer Cherry's vision of the devil became until she could physically see him, in the corner of the small classroom. He sat with his hands together, holding them against his curled smile. Then he waved. Cherry looked around her to see at whom. When she turned back to him, he nodded at her and motioned again. Terrified of making him angry, she waved back, low and small. After all, according to the teacher, he was evil and dangerous. Cherry did not want to provoke him.

"God has sent down his angels to watch over us. To be his eyes. They are like his soldiers following his every command," the teacher continued.

Another character formed on the other side of the room, opposite of where the devil sat with his sinister grin. The angel was a towering golden figure with a heavy brow that seemed to scold her. The angel of God. He must have seen her wave at the devil. She just knew he would report the transgression back to God. She would never be allowed in heaven if she made friends with the devil.

"Jesus died so that we will be saved from the grips of Satan. He has set us free. All you must do is invite him into your heart. Now everyone, bow your heads."

Cherry did as she was told.

"*Peek*," the devil whispered in her ear like a hiss. "*Make sure the angel sees you doing the right thing."*

She opened one eye to see the look of disappointment on the golden face. A long-feathered quill scribbled onto a scroll. She fell for it. That sneaky devil. Jesus was her only hope now. She would ask Jesus to live inside of her heart, like some holy possession. This would make the devil go away and get the condescending angel off her back.

Cherry raised her hand with her head bowed, and her eyes shut tight, just as the teacher instructed. Then she felt the creepy hand on her shoulder. She dared not peek again, but she knew the devil was doing something to sabotage her plan. Cherry shook with fear; tears poured from her face as she repeated the words of the teacher desperately hoping it would work and the devil would leave her alone.

Soon the hand lifted. The prayer was over. Cherry opened her eyes and quickly wiped the tears before Mitchell could see them. The devil was gone, and so was the angry angel. The ice cream lifted her mood a little, but the whole ordeal still had her shaken up. She kept the horror of the experience to herself.

All too soon, the day was over, and Cherry found herself in the still darkness of her room. She tucked herself in, fear gripping her, making it impossible to sleep. It was not long before the devil appeared, rocking in the chair with his hand together pressed against his curled smile, watching her just as he had done at the church.

"Hey, Satan," she said with a weal laugh. He knew what she tried to do. She tried to banish him away forever, but it didn't work. She must not have done it right. The teacher said Jesus would save her from her sins, but here the devil was, ready for her to make him angry again.

"So, about today, I just did that so my friend, Mitchell,

wouldn't know that I actually love you. I'll do all the bad things you tell me. I'll do whatever you want."

Without a word he disappeared. Cherry yanked the blanket over her head, "Dear God, I am so sorry I was talking to the devil, but he's super bad, and I don't want him to hurt me. Please forgive me. Please, please, PLEASE forgive me."

Cherry stayed under the blanket until she fell asleep. She dreamt of the towering golden angel walking in front of her while she followed him toward the gates of heaven. White clothes had replaced her nightgown. She thought maybe this would impress the angel, but his brow was as heavy as ever. He shook his head, as a father would before deciding a punishment, and motioned for her to sit down in a chair in front of a screen. When Cherry obeyed, a movie of her life began to play every single bad thing she had ever done: sneaking a cookie, hitting her sister, lying about doing her homework, all the bad leading up to her conversation with the devil in her bedroom. When the movie was over, the angel was gone. The gates, the pillars, everything around her began to burn, including the chair that she was stuck in. Then she started to burn. No matter how loud she screamed or how hard she tried, she could not escape what felt like an eternity of burning pain.

Cherry finally woke with a jerk, covered in sweat from the stress of her dream. Someone was knocking on her window.

"Cherry! We're late. Let's go!" Mitchell yelled at her from outside.

She was so stressed and distracted the night before; she forgot to set her alarm. With her parents already at work, she slept almost a full hour longer than she should have. Cherry dressed and quickly gathered her things for school.

She was thankful that Mitchell was her best friend and that

he had waited for her. They walked quickly in silence on the bike path which went up a hill through the pine trees for half a mile to the railroad tracks just out of sight of the school yard. They were so late; no one else was on the path.

Behind them, though, the angry angel walked with his long-feathered quill and the scroll where kept her log, adding her tardiness, no doubt. She turned her attention to the trees to distract her from her short-comings, but then she spotted him. The devil lurked behind every tree and bush she tried to focus on. Smiling his curled smile and waving as he had in the Sunday school classroom.

When Cherry and Mitchell reached the railroad tracks, the crossing guard had long been relieved of duty. Cherry heard the loud horn and could feel the vibration of the locomotive.

"It could be a long train, Cherry," the devil whispered only to her. *"You'll be even later to school. You have plenty of time to cross the tracks. Trains don't go as fast as cars."*

"But the angel is watching me. He'll tell God and know that I am friends with you."

"Are you ashamed of me, Cherry?"

Before Mitchell could ask who she was talking to, Cherry took the five steps to cross the tracks.

"What are you doing? That's dangerous," Mitchell yelled over the sound of the blaring horn getting ever closer.

"Tell him to cross, too," the devil whispered.

"No," she answered weakly.

She looked down the tracks and saw the oncoming train. Mitchell would have a little time before it reached the crossing, but it was dangerous and against the rules to cross when a train was coming.

"Tell him."

"Come on, Mitch. You can make it," Cherry encouraged weakly.

"You're crazy."

"It could be a long train, and we're going to get detention if we're any later than we are."

Mitchell stood there considering the distance of the train.

"Go now! You can make it."

"But we'll get in trouble."

"We're in trouble either way. COME ON NOW!" Cherry was crying. The angel stood behind the boy, looking into Cherry's soul. The devil stood beside the angel with his evil grin.

"No. I can't!"

"JUST GO!"

Mitchell took three steps onto the tracks. No more.

I Should Not

Mary Magdalene Gilliam was my grandmother. My father's mother. She passed away February 2015. The years leading to this moment were riddled with incoherence, frustration, and fear. Then there were moments of clarity, comfort, and the desire to hear her daughters sing. This story, inspired by her illness, became my very first published work and appeared in the international anthology COLP: The Passage of Time. *The story itself moves through time as the narrator, confused at her physical state, retraces her steps to put the pieces of her entire life back together. Again.*

I am lost. Hurt. Blood is drying down my leg. I have been injured worse before on hikes, but for some reason, my entire body seems slow and pained. I need to find help. At the end of the road, I can see a house, a white farmhouse. Surely someone there can help me. How did this happen? I have never been lost before. I am an expert navigator; ask anyone on my team.

I am a member of a hiking group and have led some of the most dangerous excursions in the country. In 1956, I led a team of five to the summit of Yosemite's Half Dome. This was on day one of our twenty-six-day journey through the Yosemite Valley to Lyell Canyon. Everyone who started, I saw to the end. How is it I can navigate a wilderness on the sole knowledge of maps, but fail to find my way back home from my own backyard? This has been my home for my entire life. I have walked these woods hundreds of times, named the trees and the rocks. These woods are my second home; I escape here when life is too much.

This morning I woke up to a beautiful sunrise, a perfect mix of pale blue, white, and yellow in the east. The weather was crisp and ideal for a hike. I chose the east entrance. With the season being mid-spring, the trees and underbrush were lush and vibrant green. Had I been anymore unfamiliar, I would not have found it. It took ten feet to see the beaten age-old path that I stomped bare, season after season. Smaller than I remember, but my path nonetheless. Every year brought new life and a familiar welcome to nature and its beauty. Birds chirped unseen in the canopy of ancient elm and maple trees easily seventy feet above me. The ground was still moist from the morning dew, and the smell of raw earth and organic decay filled me with nostalgia; like meeting an old friend for coffee.

I spent what felt like an hour just walking my path; greeting it like an old friend. I began to notice the day becoming warmer quite quickly. Looking to the canopy gave me no bearing of the time. The sun had passed its peak and clouds were threatening to hide it further than the cover of trees. When I brought my gaze down, the forest seemed strange. I felt weird. I turned once, twice, and again. I did not know the direction I had come, nor how long I had walked. Soon the sun would disappear, and I would have

I SHOULD NOT

to guess.

My heart pounded, and my breath quickened: panic. I found a space to sit. My hands shook; they did not seem like my hands. Had I eaten? Drank? What a rookie mistake to take out your door unprepared for a journey. I knew better. I also knew no one would come looking for me. No one knew I was out here. Just another rookie mistake.

I stood up, but too fast. My head became heavy, and my vision narrowed. My legs felt as if they were thick with mud as I attempted to continue my journey. I must have fallen hard.

I awoke to the drizzle of rain and the wet of the earth under me. It was dark by that time, and my entire body screamed in painful protest as I pulled myself up. My joints, muscles, even my skin seemed unhappy with my napping place. I sat upright to a seated position. Dirt and sticks embedded in my skin from the pressure of lying. Many times I have been scared. This time, the fear completely consumed me to the point of hysterics. I struggled to wipe away the dirt. I must have hit my left knee on a rock on the way down; it was still bleeding. I pulled some mud over my wound in hopes to advance the clotting. My skin was paper thin. I needed to keep moving and find my way out.

Hours more I continued slow as pain filled each step. The sun was risen again when I reached the clearing. In the morning light I could make out a dirt road on the horizon. I looked around to see if it was familiar. It was not. I was in a cow pasture. We did not own cows. The Henderson's kept cows, but this could not have been their field.

I reached the road and wanted nothing more than to run, but I could not bring my battered body to cooperate. It was another mile before I saw the house. Thank goodness.

"MRS. CUNNINGHAM!!" a man shouts, bursting from the

front porch door. Cunningham is my husband's name. Had John come here looking for me?

"Mrs. Cunningham, oh my word. Here, let me carry you." The young man bends down to pull my legs from under me.

My body gives way, but I protest, "Pardon, me! Where is John? Where is my husband?" I demand.

"Don't worry, ma'am. We are going to get you some help. Thank goodness you are alive. Let me get you inside, and we will call Trudy. She will be so relieved."

Trudy is my daughter. Why is this man not calling my husband? Trudy is still in diapers. Maybe I had bumped my head a little too hard.

The man sits me on a chair inside the house and pulls a phone from his pocket.

"Yes, my address is 31 Henderson Way."

The man walks into the other room and lowers his voice. He must be a Henderson. But this is not a Henderson house that I know.

"She is asking for her husband, so I think she is having an episode."

He keeps talking about me like I am not present, maybe physically but not mentally.

"Mrs. Cunningham, do you know where you are?"

"I'm on Henderson Property in Jefferson County Missouri."

"Yes." He spoke into the phone.

"Ma'am, do you know what today is? Or the year?" he directs these ridiculous questions at me.

"I started my walk yesterday morning, Sunday. So today is Monday, March 5th, 1960. Where is John, my husband?" I become more frustrated. The man continues to talk on the phone, and now I am done listening. Soon he returns and hands it to me.

I SHOULD NOT

"Hello?"

"Mama! It's Trudy are you okay?"

"Trudy? Who is this?" The person speaking is a grown woman. I do not know this Trudy. She is not MY Trudy.

"Mama, the ambulance is coming to get you, I will meet them where you are, and we will go to the hospital together, okay? I love you, Mom." The woman is crying. My Trudy. She is grown. My husband, John, passed away last year. I forgot my husband is gone. My daughter has to live with me and take care of me.

"Thank you, Honey. I love you, too. I will see you soon." Ashamed I hand the young man the phone.

"John died last year from lung cancer," I tell the young man, apologetically. "The doctor had given him a month; he was gone in a week. Today is May 16th, 2015. You are Nathan, my best friend's grandson, rest her soul."

I wipe a tear with my cleanest hand and look down. I know this hand. This old and wrinkled, liver-spotted and paper thin hand. It seems like in an hour I lived an entire life and not even known. My mind is melting away and my body withered along with it.

I wish I had not woken up from that spot in the woods where things seemed as they should; changing with the seasons but remaining faithfully familiar. Surely now they will confine me to four walls with eyes always watching.

I should not have woken up.

A Mirror Negative

In July 2017, I finished my very first novel. As a reward and much needed mom-vacation, I booked my first writer's retreat. Ghost Town Writer's Retreat in Georgetown, Colorado is where I met the foundation of professional friends I have today. This horror writing gathering thrust me into circles of well-established authors as well as beginners like myself.

The following story is my first attempt to write dark/ horror fiction and finding a balance between good and evil.

She moaned and shook. Lying on the cold, dank concrete in an abandoned basement. Her swollen abdomen contracted. The young woman rolled to her left and right in the pitch black. A gush of thick black liquid poured from her and onto the floor, flowing deep into cracks in the foundation, searching for something to soak, absorb, cling to. The tarry substance covered the red-inked pentagram drawn onto the ground she lay on. Legs opened wide; her once low grumble escalated into a scream of excruciating pain. From her birth canal came both light and darkness. Louder her shriek grew until a brilliant radiance along with a colorless void burst from between her thighs.

The glow fought to fill the room, banishing the damp cold and mildew from what it touched. The cherub she birthed rose into the air, stretching thick baby arms and legs. Small lips parted into a yawn and then to a smile as she looked down at her surrogate. The woman lay motionless staring at the tiny winged baby radiating purity and warmth. She raised a hand to her as a tear fell from the corner of her eye in awe and fear of the innocence before her.

The ebony waters continued to leak from her womb. In the murky pool lay a ball of thin limbs, a scant torso and a head too large in proportion to the ink colored body. Instead of a cry, a hoarse screech came from the ugly being on the floor. He was cold and only knew pain. From a still haunted corner of the room, long clawed fingers attached to thin vile arms groped the ground toward the crying pathetic mass, grabbing arms, legs, and pulling the defiled atrocity into the darkness with them.

But good was winning, faster than the condemned could retreat to their permanent darkness. Just before the greedy hands pulled the tiny demon to the place where they dwell, a ray of light touched his right knee, paling the once black surface. Then they were banished to the place where the others hide. The battle still waged between the foul wickedness of the dark void and the righteous purity of the light. The tar began to boil on the ground, hissing. It's mass ebbing and flowing in aggressive defiance. It bubbled and popped in a turbulent contest. When touched by the light, the liquid splashed into the air, licking the cherub on her right knee, leaving a black mark where the skin had once been pale.

The young woman watched in horror as the battle continued.

She feared evil would win and she would spend her eternity in the place where her tiny demon remained, to only know the pain of her actions. She also feared for purity to triumph. Certainly, she would be banished, too. She desired to be in the light with her beautiful cherub who floated and cooed above her, but the wickedness in her heart had birthed an unholy son. She deserved to follow him into the abyss.

With a flash so bright the young woman shielded her eyes, good prevailed against the horrors, cleansing the floor of the vile fluid, the pentagram faded, even dirt held no place. The cherub reached back and lifted the girl from the floor. Clean water and warmth enveloped her, cleansing her body and soul of the treachery done to her for this purpose. She was wrapped in a white cloth and lowered gently to the ground, purified and made anew. The angelic creature descended as well, into the girl's arms. Her wings faded and she nestled against the woman's breast. The light faded into a dim glow of morning. The woman was a mother. The once cherub, a helpless babe with a dark mark on her right knee.

The little girl grew and grew. She was a sweet child, listened well and loved her mother. Her birthmark, so profound against her fair skin, caused alarm. The blemish would sometimes grow and cover her entire knee. During these times, she would become increasingly mischievous. She would protest her mother, hitting and biting her. She was so young; the mother thought maybe the growing mark was painful for her daughter, making her act out. She had taken the girl to the doctor to have the spot removed, but after many attempts, the procedure always fell through. The doctor became ill when he agreed to remove the area. After weeks of waiting, the mother received a letter from the physician. He explained the mark was not harming the child. The procedure was unnecessary, and she should wait until the girl was older. Knowing the path taken to bring her into the world, the mother prayed for her daughter. Over time the mark became smaller, and the girl's behavior improved.

The boy grew tangled in the cold black limbs of the vile creatures who claimed him in the beginning but not for long. Because of the white mark on his leg, the demons lashed out at him, attacked him, clawed and bit. One day the mark grew so bright, he was ejected from the darkness and left, a thin, wiry naked child, abandoned on the cold concrete basement of his birth. Being away from the depths was painful, but in a way, was less than the tortures of his infancy. The toddler cried out.

Within minutes, the inhabitants of the home discovered the child with skin like char, bare and crying in their cellar. They wrapped him in love and took him in, but he was a difficult child. He fought every request. He screamed all hours of the night in pain without explanation or cure.

Until one day, when his new adopted parents were at the end of their rope. They had raised the boy for four years. Their marriage was falling apart, and depression had sunk its teeth deep into the fabric of their home. The curtains stayed drawn, and they lived at the mercy of the small, wiry little boy. As they prepared for yet another evening of inhuman shrieks and cries, they were met with something else entirely. One hour, then two, then another. Nervous the child succumbed to his tortures, the parents looked in on him. He was asleep. What else was peculiar, his legs peeking from the bottom of the child's long sleeping shirt, one dark as night, the other fair and pale. The white mark, once as small as a nickel, covered his entire leg.

A MIRROR NEGATIVE

By the age of five, the girl had been expelled from school. Without focused psychological counseling, she could not return. The mother advocated for her daughter, but she knew as her birthmark grew, so did something deep inside of her - something just as dark as the mark. Just behind her eyes brewed pure evil. Even in summer, she dressed her to cover the spot as it grew across her back and began down her other leg. The darkness was consuming her, and even the mother's strongest prayers were no match. The evil was like a flame, and the girl enjoyed fanning it.

He woke to his alarm and dressed for school before his parents emerged from their room. He was thankful for the season where his pain was minimal and his mood bright. As he moved through the house to the kitchen for breakfast, he pulled open the curtains to allow the morning sun to shine in his home, in his heart. He could feel the darkness diminished a little more. In college, he still got into fights, still plotted against the others who made fun of his skin, still smeared the reputations of his exes. But the darkness in him was far overpowered by his light.

In the hall, he noticed his reflection as he passed the mirror. His hair, skin, even his eyes once so dark they appeared as black holes into his soul, had turned to stark white as a blanket of fresh snow. His heart was full of light and love, and he was not afraid. He had overcome the evil from which he was born.

The boy went to school that day. He walked through the courtyard where students shuffled to classes. He felt the cold approaching. Not the temperature outside but the freezing pain he had felt as a child living with demons. He heard the shots within his chest. They rang out muting the screams around him. Then he saw her. She had not fired yet, but he knew her intent. He read hatred in her mind. He recognized the deep hue covering her being. It was his. The malevolence had consumed her as the light saturated him. His comfort and love came at the price of hers. She had no love left within her, just the profound pain he had lived his entire life.

He was not afraid. He walked as she planned where to shoot into the crowd. His light, his balance. He knew what needed to happen to save the lives around him.

She felt him approach and shunned it as she turned to the albino boy. He knew what she was there to do. He saw the wicked in her, the scene which was to unfold. He thought he could stop her. He was wrong. The pale skinned boy, the kind she was born as, seemed to float toward her in the crowded courtyard of her former college, having been barred and banished from the grounds. She would show them, but first, she would show him.

The pale boy walked towards the girl with skin that seemed to swallow even the sunlight, lost in its depth. The air stilled. From within her purse, she pulled the gun and pointed. He kept walking. And like a snap of a twig, a crack of lightning, a blink of an eye, the gun fired.

Both dark and light fell to the ground as equals.

His name publicized, immortalized, exploited. Hers repeated by those who knew her, which was few -the girl with the strange skin and mean streak. Her heroic act was not typical of her cold nature. Not celebrated as the hero she was, but fast forgotten in the slew of propaganda and smeared with fear and hate for the boy who took her life.

A Love Denied

I enjoy a nice cozy romance every now and then, but very little of my stories have anything to do with relationships. To date you will not even find a single sex scene in my books. They make me nervous and I am always self-conscious of what my friends and family would think of my take on contemporary love. Here is my PG, gushy little love scene.

She noticed his blatant staring from the corner of her eye, but ignored him. The factory workers who stopped at the small super market for their lunch on the way to work often gawked at the city girl picking up eggs and milk for the day.

"I would catcall you, but you know how to kill people."

Pretending not to hear him, she continued her path into the store. Hush fell over the patrons as she passed, eyes forward, never down.

Now, who in their right mind? She thought, a smirk playing at the corner of her mouth. Her resume was no secret in this place. Hell, the town was so small they knew about her entire life before she even unhitched the moving trailer. Ten years of military service and a failed marriage brought this Denver girl back to Morganfield, Kentucky.

But that voice had no accent. No southern drawl. She should have looked. Hopefully he was gone before she finished.

"Cash, check, or debit, sweetie?"

"Cash, Ms. Sue. Always cash."

A set of muscles wearing a hat started bagging her groceries.

"Oh, I have my own bags. Please. Use these."

She fought with the bundle to release a single bag for him. She held it out avoiding eye contact. Muscles in hats rarely needed more attention than she was willing to give. Waiting long enough to realize he was not taking the bag from her she set it down and looked back at Ms. Sue for help.

"Honey, he don't work here."

Heat rose up her neck to her cheeks and she prayed she could leave before the hives became more evident.

The hat wearing pile of muscle also had a smile. A familiar one.

"You're either going to help me, or let me do it myself."

The man laughed, accepted her discarded bag, and continued working.

Anna stared at him, unable to rationalize this man finding her in the haystack of nowhere Kentucky.

Mr. Jeff, as she called her best friend Emily's, dad, cleared his throat in line behind her. Speaking so even the factory audience could hear, "Do you know him, Anna? Is he bothering you?"

"No, and no," She said to the older gentleman.

Sue handed the Anna her change. She folded a couple of bills and offered them to the man.

"Oh, this is full service," he stood presumptuously close to her after over a decade apart. "I'll carry these out for you."

Anna swallowed the pulse from her throat and waved a comforting hand at Mr. Jeff before leading the muscle outside.

"He'll shoot you before I do," she joked, refusing to look at him until her pounding heart and butterfly stomach was under control. She knew things about the man helping her likely few women knew. They had been children of sorts, clumsy, naïve. His eyes were friendly and his smile, warm and familiar. She memorized his features years ago. Then he married. Years later so did she. He was forgotten.

"What are you doing here?"

"I think you know why I am here."

"Because you're obsessed with me and stalked me across the country to my favorite grocery store to profess your undying love and threaten to kill yourself if I don't agree be with you?"

"No, you asshole." No one would have guessed he was not from a neighboring town. His jeans and dirty fitted ball cap could have been Morganfield's uniform. Andrew rubbed his neck and said nothing else. His bicep obvious in his t-shirt, not stretching the fabric but threatening to, made Anna hyper aware of her own physique. After two kids, she was not in the shape she was in her twenties. This sudden realization gave her a foothold on her overly hopeful emotions.

"What are you doing here?" she pressed again, looking around for town gossipers.

Ms. Sue was likely on the phone giving a running commentary to the bunko club. The ladies at the hair salon across the street peeked through mini-blinds, holding up their phones and recording the entire interaction to share on the neighborhood social media site. Anna knew the headlines all too well: *Ms. Norton's*

Mystery Man. She had enough unsolicited publicity for just moving back. Owning the only Bed and Breakfast for fifty miles could have been dubbed a crime by how many married women dubbed her business a whore house. A divorced mom of two had to do something for an income, but prostitution was not one of them.

"Well, I thought I'd come see you."

"But why are you *here?*" she finally stepped closer to him.

Andrew put the bags down gently and closed the remaining distance. She hugged him back, eyes closed wanting so much for this moment to not be a dream. She held her arms around his chest, because he was too tall to reach over his shoulders. He smelled clean, though no cologne. He was as awkward as she remembered, but still easy on the eyes.

"Your friend said you were here," he said pressing his cheek to her head.

"I hate you so much," she said when she released him.

"Rude. And a lie."

She picked up a bag leaving one for him to carry, "Did you want to get something?"

"No, I ate at your place."

"You're staying at the B and B?"

"Where else would I stay? In my defense I didn't even know you owned it until I got here. Had a nice chat with Emily."

Anna cocked her head and gave no expression though his laughing eyes made her melt inside.

"You're a stalker."

"You stopped writing me. Kels let me know what happened and that you'd moved back so I figured I'd swing by on my way to training. See how you were doing." He opened her door for her.

"You know I'm fine, Andrew." She faced him for a moment, took the bag out of his hand and closed the car door. "I pushed you away because our conversations always seemed one sided."

"You were married, Anna. I didn't want to be the reason it didn't work. Hell, I wish you and Raul did work out so you wouldn't have to go through the pain of ending your marriage. If anyone knows how shitty divorce is, it's me."

"You knew. You knew all these years all you had to do was breathe like you wanted me. Nothing's changed. I stopped writing to you because it was obvious this would never be what I wanted it to be." Anna fell silent when she realized she was almost yelling. "My marriage was running on borrowed time, but I was starting to imagine you as a backup plan. Even admitting that is ridiculous. That's why, even after, I never contacted you again. You were so adamant about never marrying again and being alone that I knew I wasn't being fair to myself. So, please tell me, why are you here?"

"Anna, I love you. I knew it back then and ignored it. I made up that bullshit so you wouldn't think I was trying to break up your marriage to be with you. When you stopped writing I actually started to believe it. If I had one more chance at a real life, it would be with you. I was stupid to break your heart then. I've thought about you every day since."

"Dammit, I hate you." Anna got into her car and left him in the parking lot.

"A lie!" he called after her, smiling as he climbed into his truck.

Dirty Bombs

In October 2007, I deployed to Iraq for the first time. I spent the fifteen months resolved to the fact I would just live there forever. This mentality kept me from over anticipating the journey home and made the length bearable. I do not recall doing much reading except one book. Sergeant Clise gave me his copy of World War Z *by Max Brooks. This opened a door for intense nightmares and long stares into darkness considering the parallel universe of zombies in a war zone. Where would I go? Who could I trust? Over a decade later, I finally found the courage to pen my first zombie story.*

Her ears rang, disorienting her after the blast hit right outside. She blinked through the darkness, small rays of light shined through the holes that peppered her roommate's side of the metal trailer. Miranda rolled softly to the floor, dragged her body armor from its resting place under her twin bed and pulled it open over her. She low crawled to the growing pool of blood by the other twin bed. Christy appeared to be still sleeping peacefully, her pulse nonexistent. Miranda lay for a moment listening. More impacts followed the loud whistles of bombs as the enemy continued their assault on the forward operating base. Though they shook her to the core, the blasts moved farther and farther away - mortars. The enemy must have been targeting the embassy.

Fumbling to find her roommate's gear. She secured an extra medic pouch, a full combat load of ammunition, and the spare set of keys to the hospital compound. She considered taking her friend's weapon, but she knew how rarely Christy cleaned it.

Bold enough to stand, Miranda, moved her armor over her head, feeling the wound for the first time. In her grey shirt, she found a hole the size of a pencil eraser. She pushed her finger into her abdomen and felt the sharp piece of shrapnel. A sigh of relief it had not even penetrated the muscle. The metallic thorn would have to stay until she made it safely to the combat support hospital where she would prepare to treat the more severely wounded.

Kevlar helmet and body armor secured, she fought against the pain to pull up her uniform pants and lace her boots. The embedded noncommissioned officer within her cringed at the mismatched uniform, but there was little time. She threw the rest of her uniform in an assault pack, with the extra rounds and medic pouch. One thirty-round magazine slid with ease into the ammo well of her rifle, a short motion slammed it into place, and she chambered a round.

Her hand touched the doorknob, and a gasp came from the bed across the room.

"Jenkins!" Miranda whispered a startled cry. But something was off. For a moment she considered her assessment had been flawed, but no. Her friend was lifeless without breath or pulse for over two minutes. "Jenkins?"

At the sound of her voice, the corpse fell off the bed. Legs unmoving, the body crawled across the floor to her. Miranda moved quickly around it, pinning the base of the neck with her boot. Two fingers reached for the neck. There was no pulse.

"You have got to be fucking kidding me." She pulled a knife from its sheath attached to her armor and with a short pendulum swing of her arm, pushed the blade into Christy's temple. The body went limp.

The bombs stopped. The enemy had not, in fact, targeted the embassy, but meant to pepper the living areas with their contaminated weapons. Remembering her wound, she sat a moment to collect herself and check her state of being.

Her heart pounded inside of her chest. Adrenaline courses through her body. Growls came from neighboring rooms. She had enough food and water to last two days if she rationed, but if there was any escape or treatment, her chances would pass her by if she stayed to scavenge for more.

She tightened the chin strap of her helmet and kept the knife in her trigger hand. For the first time in her career, she wished she had a bayonet. With 210 rounds readily accessible and another 210 in her assault pack, one-shot one-kill could still end quickly in close quarters combat. The forward operating base held 25,000 soldiers and countless civilians. Ammo would run out before targets did.

The hospital would hold the largest collection of dead, but it was a secured compound. Miranda knew every turn, corner, and room and could evade for the half mile it took to get to the back gate.

The door resisted her push to open. Swallowing her adrenaline, her fear, she guided the lock as slow and soft as she could.

Any more drama in this situation and she would come undone.

"You can cry when it's over," she whispered and flipped off the switch within her governing her emotions. She was no longer Miranda, mother of an eighteen-month-old named Naomi in Rutland, Vermont. She was Staff Sergeant St Clair, and had a mission.

Silence. To the left and right of her, nothing moved. Her boots crunched the gravel at the foot of the steps that led to her room. She inhaled deeply and breathed it out of her mouth, a slow and quiet force.

Running, she calculated her pace. Exactly four minutes to reach the gate. If open, the walls surrounding the compound would offer her fast cover if anything pursued. But it would also mean things within the hospital were far worse off.

When she passed the tall, concrete Texas barriers designed to shield the living areas from attacks, she saw others. Some running, the dead dragging.

Thank God Brad Pitt was wrong. They don't run, she thought, jumping a shallow dry ditch, in sight of the gate. Closed and locked. A familiar face was behind it.

"Conrad, open the damn gate!" There was no recognition in the young soldier's stance. He swayed back and forth.

"Shit," Miranda whispered, lowering her M4 rifle. Slowed to a walk, she approached making sure there were no threats on her side of the fence.

Then she was face to face with the young man. He worked in the headquarters building on night shift and was promoted, having pinned a rocker under his previous mosquito-winged ranked the day before. She grabbed his collar through the gate, pressing his forehead against the bars. Not happy to use his eye socket as an entry point, she doubted any of her comrades would get open casket funerals either way.

The gate was closed but not secured. Miranda shouldered her rifle and opened the soldered bar door. She cleared the immediate area before turning to lock the entrance.

"Sar'nt St. Clair!" A group of five soldiers ran from the living area toward the gate. Three more trailed behind, one supported by the other two.

She waited, keeping eyes and ears open to the inner courtyard she was standing near and the area that closed between her and the group.

"Fucking zombies, Garrett. Jenkins turned into a goddam zombie."

The six-foot-three bald man helped the others inside and looked down at Private First Class Conrad's body.

"Top, too," he said with a long sigh. "First Sar'nt was hit with shrapnel in his damned sleep."

Miranda nodded. "Who's that?"

"Sar'nt Hutch from the OR. She's got a deep one on her shin. Down to the bone. She put a fucking tourniquet on herself."

"Take her to the ER," Miranda shouted to the two soldiers helping the injured woman. "You three work in maintenance, right?"

The junior soldiers nodded.

"I need you to clear the compound. Lockdown as you go. Let in survivors and send them to the outpatient clinic. That's where we'll keep the manpower pool. I'm sure you knuckleheads have played enough video games to know what to do. They might be your superior, but if they are already dead, you need to stab them in the head. Try not to kill anyone that has a chance, even if they're assholes. Got it?"

"Roger, Sar'nt." With that, the three soldiers went on their mission.

"I'll help you clear the TOC," Miranda said looking up at the superior noncommissioned officer. "You're taking charge, eh?"

Master Sergeant Garrett pulled the 9mm handgun from his leg holster, and they made their way to the headquarters building. As they rounded the corner to the entrance, Miranda saw where a rocket hit the top of the tall concrete barrier. Fresh rubble was scattered everywhere, and there by the door was a large puddle of blood. Drops led to Conrad's body.

Garrett punched in a series of numbers, and a light above the door handle turned green, granting them access. Miranda flipped her safety switch and gave him a nod. He swung the door open.

"Clear," Miranda said staring down the dark empty hallway.

RAP RAP RAP! Garrett pounded on the wall. "You guys okay in here?"

Tap Tap Tap. She heard it, faint and far down the hall toward the locked tactical operations room.

Garrett nodded back to Miranda, and she followed him in, listening. He pushed another set of numbers and opened the door to the TOC.

"Get off the damn floor, Sar'nt Viola, Jesus Christ."

Sergeant First Class Viola huffed as she crawled out from under her desk.

"I think that boy is dead," the older woman shook a finger toward Conrad's empty desk.

"Yeah, no shit. Get the COMS up. Call a medevac to Baghdad. We need to get out of here." Garrett turned to Miranda. "I got this. Run to the ER. Send two troops back here from manpower. We'll run accountability the best we can. You good?"

Miranda nodded again. "Yeah, just find us a way out of here."

As she made her way to the main hospital building, she

spotted the team of three.

"What's the status?" she yelled to the young soldiers.

"We're secured, Staff Sergeant, just scanning the gate for survivors."

"I need one of you in here with Master Sergeant Garrett. Top's out. Garrett's in charge."

Without hesitation, one man broke into a light jog and disappeared into the headquarters building.

The moment she opened the outer door, she heard the screams. She unbuckled her chin strap and made her way to her office in the outpatient side of the hospital. She set her assault pack on the floor and put her armor on the rack. Miranda pulled her shirt over her head, her wound still bleeding. Her fingers dug inside, grabbing with her fingernails, and she pulled out the metal thorn. Her wound cleaned and patched with gauze and tape, she put on the clean shirt from her bag. On her desk was a picture of her and her newborn daughter.

Miranda inhaled deeply, her heart threatening to pull her apart. She picked up her rifle and assault pack and made her way to the emergency room.

"If you are uninjured and not a medic, I need you to move to the outpatient clinic and await an assignment," she announced into the crowded bay of makeshift beds. All three mesh litters had a person in them. The first of which was a CPR in progress.

Miranda pulled back the curtain, just as the body reanimated, grabbing the specialist doing chest compressions, Miranda slid her blade into its temple.

"Major Morales?" she called out.

"Not accounted for, Sergeant."

"Who's the doc on duty?"

"I am," a meek voice came from the next curtain. Captain

Rainey was a pediatrician from Las Vegas.

"Ma'am? You're one rotation?"

The doctor shook her head. Miranda and the doctor had bonded over the last few months, having left their children with relatives to deploy.

"Okay. We're okay," Miranda projected her voice over the commotion behind the last curtain. "Listen up. MSG Garrett is in charge and working on getting all of us on a medevac out of here. We're all getting the fuck out of here. But, this will sound crazy. We're dealing with a zombie epidemic." She paused, hearing herself say the words. "We will assume everything we've seen on TV to be true. Triage will be slightly different as well."

The yelling in the back of the bay was increasing. Fully prepared to slice everyone, Miranda pulled back the curtain. Four soldiers held down a large local, national man who was thrashing despite being restrained. His eyes were yellow and his skin grey.

"Johnson, he's dead. Grab that scalpel and…"

The soldier did not wait for her to finish. Silence fell over the room finally.

A young red-haired soldier released her grip on the dead man. Her sleeve was red with blood. A U shape grew on the cloth. Terror on her face, she looked up to Miranda, her leader, and mentor.

"Get a tourniquet on that now!"

Johnson again took action. He coached the fellow soldier through the placement and even the pain as he wrenched it down as tight as he could, just above her elbow.

"Sar'nt St. Clair!" a voice yelled from the hallway.

Miranda met the soldier she had sent to the TOC, "Yeah?"

"ETA is thirty minutes. We only have four birds coming at a time. Master Sergeant Garrett says only uninjured soldiers can go on the first round. That's 44 seats, Sergeant. We have positive accountability on 65. They can't all go."

She pulled the back of her hand over her brow, "I'll have them ready."

"Ma'am, please hand your 9mm to Specialist O'Flynn."

The red-haired girl looked at her perplexed.

"Johnson, I need you and Captain Rainey to come with me and help triage the folks in the outpatient clinic. O'Flynn," Miranda stepped close to her soldier. "I need you to hold it down in here, okay? I know you're injured, but you will run a tight ship for a few minutes until I get back. Continue to triage in here and send the uninjured to the clinic. I'm not leaving you. Okay?"

"Yes, Sergeant."

Once the three of them reached the empty hallway just shy of the outpatient clinic, Miranda stopped them.

"They are sending a medevac, but we won't all fit."

"I'll stay," Johnson said without skipping a beat.

"No, you're going. That's an order, Johnson. I swear to God too many people have already died."

"With all due respect, Sergeant. I'll make sure they all make it out."

Miranda did not want to argue. She knew Johnson too well. He should have been a Ranger instead of a medic.

"Well then, Ma'am, we need to triage everyone. Make them tell you of any injuries they have. No open wounds are to leave on that bird. We can't risk infecting other FOBs, especially the Green Zone. They only have 44 seats on the birds, but, honestly, I don't give a fuck. If we have 63 healthy people, they are all leaving on that medevac. Now I have to grab something from my office. You guys get started and have everyone assemble in here. I'll be there in a minute."

Miranda unlocked the door to her office and shut it behind her. She held her breath, picked up the landline phone sitting on her desk and put it to her ear. Exhale. A dial tone. Her fingers flew, punching in the numbers to make an international call.

"Andy?"

"Mark, I need you listen to me."

"And, do you know what time it is? I have to be at work in four hours."

"Dammit just listen. The hospital was hit, and the base is under attack."

"Oh my God, are you okay?"

"Yes and no," she choked on the words. "Honey, I love you so very much. And Naomi. I need to hear her. Can you wake her?"

"Ummm," Mark paused.

"I just need to hear her one last time."

"I'm, uh, not at home, Andy."

"What? What do you mean?"

"Nay is at my mom's tonight."

"Where are you?" Miranda heard a voice. Not her husband's voice. A woman's voice. Miranda slowly placed the handset back down on the receiver. Picking it back up, her hand shaking, she dialed her mother-in-law. The phone just rang, for an eternity it felt like before going to voicemail. She tried two more times, with the same voice claiming "Please leave your message for..."

"Naomi, it's your mama. I know you're too little to understand, but maybe someday you'll hear this message. I will not stop fighting until I am back home. I will do whatever it takes, to my very last breath to get back to you, my sweet little baby. And if I don't just know it's not because I gave up. I will never give up. I love you so so so so much."

A knock came at her door before it opened. Garrett ducked his head in and waited for her to collect herself.

"I'm staying back," he announced quietly.

"Me, too," she sniffed and raised her uniform blouse to reveal the small spot of blood leaking through her tan t-shirt.

"I pulled Johnson aside. He's going to create a diversion with a handful of grenades we had in the armory. The sound of the birds will draw the dead, so we must pick off stragglers and divert other survivors inside the compound. Colonel Montgomery said they'd send another round about an hour after them."

"Sounds promising," she answered, trying her best to forget what had just happened on the phone.

"The mortar rounds were tainted. The shrapnel is infecting people and then the bites after that. Is that a bite?"

"Shrapnel from my trailer."

"Well, maybe it's not infected and just a piece of tin from the walls."

"Let's get these folks ready." Miranda stood and followed Garrett into the waiting room where sixty people stood, including Sergeant First Class Viola.

"Break up into even groups of four. This is your chalk group. You will only have seconds to get on. They won't wait for you to strap in so hold on to one another for dear life."

Officers, enlisted, young and old were all getting another chance at survival. Some married with kids, others, just kids themselves. It did not matter. She was doing the right thing. Even if she survived all the way home, if she turned then, she shuttered to think of the danger she was to her own baby. The baby she'd weaned from her breast just a week before deploying.

"Staff Sergeant St. Clair and I will take positions on the roof of the ER and take out anything that might hinder this mission. You very well might need to take out some of the dead in the short distance between the bay doors and the helipad. Aim for the head and do NOT hesitate. Make it home so that our sacrifice is not in vain. Understand?"

"Yes, Master Sergeant," the room answered in a sober refrain.

Etched

Shauna wiped soapy water from the young woman's slender rib cage, sending skin into goose-flesh chills. Removing the excess ink revealed the sharp illustration of a songbird in a wisp of exaggerated ivy vines. The girl stood from the padded black leather bench and skipped to the mirror, squealing. Shauna shot the girl her best acknowledging smile to be pleasant, but her side burned under her shirt as her skin rose in the same design as the young woman's tattoo. The pain was as addictive as practicing her art.

Shauna closed the blinds to her tattoo booth and pulled up her shirt. The fresh ink of the same song bird bore a bold contrast to her other tattoos, but the new vibrant colors were a welcome variation from her traditional style. From neck to wrists, Art covered Shauna's body, each work in various stages of fading. For every tattoo she etched onto someone else, the identical image developed in the same place on herself. Unlike her paying canvases, her tattoos faded after a year of being placed, and she never overlapped her art. When ink covered every inch of her body, she waited for her oldest tattoo to disappear before accepting another commission.

Shauna Green was a leader on the New Orleans tattoo scene. Her art was recognizable and sought after for being perfect in design and technical skill. The shop where she rented a booth housed three other capable artists, but none came close to her talent. Kept to herself, hated small talk, and paid her booth rent on time every month, Shauna did not complain even when they raised her rent to a percent of her commission.

Tattooing was not a job to her as much as an everyday experiment of her strange condition. In the beginning, the first time she put a line into a person's skin, she felt it immediately. The burn of the needle. She gave enough free tattoos in a week to cover her entire back. Then she got picky, taking smaller commissions on arms and legs. By the time she filled the remaining space on her body, her back was clear. Her body was a revolving canvas.

Big Bobby, the owner of the shop, scouted her and offered Shauna a two-year apprenticeship. The study only lasted two months before clients asked for her work. Big Bobby gave her the booth in the shop's front, and because of her reputation she picked what, where, and who she tattooed, passing clients to other artists. This helped to maintain a positive work environment. That and Big Bobby claimed her pretty face in the window attracted more customers than his grand (massive) physique.

With guns cleaned and her station tidied, Shauna opened the blinds again. A man stood outside looking in on her, but he had not seen her shirt up, had he? With a smirk, he walked away. Curious eyes peered into the window all the time. On the weekends, a group of regulars would watch her through the glass. Up and coming artists would study and take notes of her technique. Journalists and photographers would harass Big Bobby for an interview with her. He no longer bothered asking her to comply, because the answer never changed. Tourists were easy to spot, snapping pictures with their smart phones or oversized tablets. There was no doubt she brought in a lot of business, but she had gotten pickier with her subjects. She was running out of room and it would be another month before she had any to spare. All that was left was a small space on the back of her shoulder blade three inches in diameter.

It was rounding out midnight. Closing time. Shauna dodged a bible verse, a pirate ship, and a viper eating a rat; she gave those to Big Bobby and the other artists. Her booth had been clean for hours and she was about to give up on the night. The store's front door chimed, signaling a potential client entering the shop. A tall man stood in the lobby. Though he wore a suit, a few dark lines were visible around his neck and wrists. His eyes worked her over. From her wrists, to her flat stomach that shown from her low-cut jeans revealing her work. As his gaze moved over her, she pulled her shirt down to cover her stomach.

"We close in an hour."

"Mine won't take long. It's just this," he said and held up a glass box. Inside was a piece of preserved paper with a small symbol. It was a simple drawing. A square with dissecting lines creating smaller squares and triangles inside. It looked like something a student would doodle on notebook paper. It required no skill or effort.

"I'm closed up for the night and the guys already have clients. Come back tomorrow. I'm sure one of them can fit you in," She said to the man.

She turned away, but the man grabbed her by the arm. He was stronger than what his suit revealed. Despite her own strength, he turned her around with little effort. Instinctively with her free hand, she reached to the back of her belt and pulled her knife loose. He grabbed her wrist as she swung the knife and pulled her close into him. His chest was hard under his shirt, and it almost knocked the breath out of her.

"You will do this tattoo. It will be exactly like it is in the drawing. And you will do it now. This…" He pressed a large stack of money into her free hand. "… is ten thousand dollars cash."

If money had never been a motivation, it was that night. The man released her and followed her into the booth. While she readied her machine, he walked to the windows and closed the three sets of blinds.

"Bashful?" Shauna huffed, rolling her eyes. Ten thousand would hold her over the few months while more space cleared on her skin, maybe longer if she wanted to take on a larger piece of art. "You know you should keep your fucking hands to yourself when you want people to do stuff for you, like put permanent fucking marks on your body. I'm a goddam person, not a slave."

He did not respond. He faced her and buttoned his white collar shirt to reveal black ink in different styles and ages. She placed the tattoo on the only space she had left, which was the only bare space on his skin. She was angry, but the more she dug into his flesh, the more hers tore and bled beneath her shirt. No one knew of her affliction, but giving the punk what he deserved was worth suffering in silence. The tattoo was minor and simple compared to the rest of the work he wore on his body. When she finished, he silently slid his shirt back on, took his coat and left. Shauna released her breath at the sound of the bell.

Shauna heard Big Bobby and the others lock up and head out for the night. Being left in the shop alone never scared her, but the whole interaction with her last client had shaken her. The ten thousand dollars was far too much for what she gave him and the money weighed her bag down in a way that sickened her stomach. Something was not right. She stepped out the back door and looked up and down the alley where she had parked her motorcycle. Empty. She set down the trash and locked the door.

A force slammed her body into the door, pinning her against it. A hand gripped the back of her shirt, pulling it back ripping the scab from her fresh mark, her collar choking her. The chilled night air blew over the fresh blood on her shoulder. She struggled against the weight to no avail. A flash of light, a camera? Then everything was black. A black fabric bag fell over her head and blocked her vision.

Everything was dark. She heard the vehicle door slide open. Whoever was there for her bound her hands behind her back with a zip tie, but she did not struggle. Being blind folded distorted her judgment of time. Had an hour past? Maybe just a few minutes before the vehicle slowed, made a few turns one after another and stopped. Shauna was led in silence into a building. Her tattoos. This had to be about her condition. They cut her clothes off, all of them. Then a series of snap and draws of a camera worked its way around her. She kept her jaw clenched, pushing the fear from her mind. Would they rape her now? Kill her? Did the man who roughed her up in the shop orchestrate all of this? They must have checked her shoulder knowing what they would find.

"Stand," commanded a distorted mechanical voice. She obeyed. Fabric touched her leg. "Put these on."

Panties, then sweatpants. A blanket was wrapped around her shoulders.

"Sit."

She sat.

"Do not remove your cover until you hear the click of the lock."

They cut away the thin plastic binding her hands. A door shut. The lock slammed. Shauna removed the black cloth from over her face. She was in a cell with one way in and one way out. There were no windows, just a bench, a tiny water faucet with a simple lever and a drain in the floor. A small piece of black charcoal on the floor in one of the four corners.

Three meals a day, she spent her time drawing on the walls, floor, ceiling of her cell. She counted the time by the fading of her marks. The last of which was the square on her shoulder she could not see and the vibrant colored song bird on her ribs.

On the day the color faded completely away, the door opened. The light was so bright she could not see the faces of the people who bound her hands and covered her face. In a vehicle for what felt like seconds compared to the time spent alone, they stopped and pulled her out. Hands unbound, cover lifted. They drove away and left her in the dark, in the alley behind her shop. Her bag at her feet. Ten million dollars inside. She took the bag, walked away, and never tattooed again.

A Foot Off The Ground

I was inspired this by the lovely Donna Munro at a flash fiction workshop to write a creepy little short while attending the Ghost Town Writers Retreat. Equipped with strange pictures, we were told to choose one. I sat by this one of a levitating girl and began writing the story from the moment I sat down.

Angela Gibbons caused her family a fright from the moment she was conceived. While in her mother's womb each week would go by, causing her mother very unusual symptoms. Little Angie was born on August 17th, 1972 at 11:23pm. Hours later, when the nurses did their nightly rounds at exactly 2:15am, they found the babe flowing exactly one foot above her assigned crib. Once they were brave enough to approach the child, no amount of force could ground her. As quickly as she rose, at 2:16am she lowered gently back to her bed. And so it was every single night.

Later it was realized, after months of studying the phenomenon, Angela Gibbons consistently levitated exactly one foot from where she lay at exactly 2:15am for exactly one minute. For months they tried to tie her down, but no matter how heavy, everything they attached to her would levitate exactly one foot off the ground at exactly 2:15am for exactly one minute every single night.

When Angie got to be seven years old, she pleaded with her parents to remove the rope from her while she slept. The heavier the object, the more tired she was the next day. It was affecting her studies at school. They reluctantly agreed, but someone had to stay and watch over her every night at exactly 2:15am for exactly one minute. After a month they were comfortable that she would go no higher than exactly one foot from her bed and allowed her to sleep without watchful eyes.

For three years Angie lived as a normal child aside from her nocturnal flights. Until she disappeared. With the doors and windows locked tight, no one had any idea where Little Angie could have gone. Authorities, being privy to her odd condition, did not spend much time or resources searching for her. They checked her tree house, the neighborhood park, and her friend's houses, all of which were unfruitful.

It was not until years later when her parents were preparing to sell their home after giving up hope for her return. A few friends of the family came to help them repair damage on the roof, they found Angie's shoe hanging from the highest point of the chimney just out of sight from the ground.

The Executioner

I am probably wrong to assume men don't have feelings but shutting them off helps me kill with a clear conscious.

"No, mister. Please don't. Pluh-lee-hee-hee-heeez."

Her hands are tied and unable to wipe the snot from pooling on her upper lip, or clean up the black smears of mascara running down her slapped-raw cheeks. Not by me. I'm not the rough 'em up type. No. I'm the closer. The last face they see. I don't see her, though. I see a job. A hefty deposit into an untraceable account.

Her husband is the target, though. He's the one with the bounty, tied to a chair behind her, face twisted in grief with swollen eyes. They make this too easy for me. Whatever his transgression with my client, the cost was much more than broken bones and additional threats of violence. His price wasn't his life, either. This was reserved for nobodies, witnesses, and cost way less than my going rate. I was paid to carve a piece of him out. Something irreplaceable. Her.

"Bay-bee." He dribbled blood from his mouth. His jaw slack, undoubtedly broken.

This sparks a louder screech from his wife, and I am done

being dramatic. She's thin enough my tool, a long thin spike, only requires half its length to penetrate her heart. A small puncture is all that's needed for her to bleed out in a little less than a minute. This is when the true hysterics begin. Torturous, yes, but I find slight comfort in thinking they have time to make peace with each other. Call me a romantic, but nothing brings a couple together like one of them dying while the other watches. Hallmark has nothing on the palpable regret exchanged between the two.

She chokes a little and I know I nicked the lung, too. Makes no difference in the grand scheme of my allotment, but I like to be precise. Shock from blood loss is a far more comfortable way to die than drowning in your own blood. This is the shred of sympathy I give my victims. I'm still human after all.

When the wife slumps over I wait an added fifteen seconds. This is usually when the target hurls threats. He'll find me and kill everyone I love. I know the cycle of grief, so I let them vent, knowing it's not personal. Besides, most people lose consciousness before they completely lose their pulse and I need the time to confirm the kill.

"I know you, John Smith. I'll fucking find you."

My disguise is quite famous, but he has no idea who I am. So, I look at him. Truly look at him for the first time. His hair cut, suit pants and torn dress shirt. The length of his finger nails, the brand of his shoe. He's a government official. Even so, my real identity is ironclad.

If you need a discreet and untraceable contract kill, you contact my alias: John Smith. If you needed a trust fund daughter of a Nobel Prize winning scientist, you called me: Sylvia Gardner.

No pulse. I turn to the target and deliver my one liner. I started doing this to solidify my alter ego as a genuine person and not just a disguise. No one would suspect a woman after hearing a man's voice.

"Thank you. This is my retirement kill." Means absolutely nothing and I say it to everyone. I'm only thirty-five. Granted, I have enough money to retire, I like my job. Two kills a year on average provides a comfy living.

Fifteen years ago, Dr. Gerald Norman Gardner, my father, developed technology for the CIA. Among his many contributions was a tiny silicone device which could disguise an agent and remove all personal identifiable markers, allowing them to assume the full identity of someone else. Voice, finger prints, blood type, hair, teeth, even their scent. Anything anyone could use to prove an identity could be altered.

This technology is how I've stayed in the business for almost a decade. The federal government thinks I have a stalker ex-boyfriend who makes contract kills every time he stops in for a visit. I play the roll well. Scared trust fund girl makes a call to Daddy who wires her money to relocate. Of course, the wire transfer is my client's payment with the relocation fee included. This might be an elaborate cover, but the charade has worked time and again.

From the wife hit in San Diego, I moved to rustic Memphis, Tennessee and was followed pretty close by the FBI. My money goes far here, and I took some time off to lose the heat. Took about three years. Long enough for me to consider finding a hobby aside from people watching at the Peabody Hotel, a job maybe. This idea is always short lived. I don't work well with others. I kill people for money. Imagine what I'd do to someone who annoyed me. This small city is a dump. Something about the mildew smell of corn at dusk helps me forget the raw chicken odor of blood. Living in Memphis is much like cleansing the pallet of anything resembling luxury. The Peabody is pretty nice though.

I opened my bookings for a new contract before bed last night and soon I'll be moving again. Today, I might find myself someone to play with while I wait. Hotels are good spots for flings. Relationships only complicated things, so anyone who gets too clingy will be informed of my psycho ex-boyfriend who will certainly kill him if he stays around long enough to meet John Smith. I'll try to find someone without the mouthy hick accent of Appalachia. Sounds like their tongues catch every vowel from escaping beyond the teeth and instead swallow them back down again. They turn words like Louisville in to a gargle.

I opt for a knee-length, floral dress with pockets. I thought I saw someone at the grocery store with a similar one and she didn't draw any attention to herself. Sunglasses are a must. I pluck them off the table by the door along with my wallet. Despite my playful mood, I maintain a stoic posture as I walk through the automatic turnstile doors and straight to the bar. Malcom pours and sits the chardonnay on the counter before I I'm within polite speaking distance to order. He nods. I nod and lay a bill on the counter before removing the glass. I don't smile even though I greatly appreciate his anticipation.

John is more charismatic. He would sit at the bar and know Malcom's life story by the end of his drink. Playing John was far less invasive than being a woman. No one touched him without permission or assumed he owed them anything in exchange for a drink or friendly conversation. John has nothing to lose. I, on the other hand, keep a stone cold façade.

"Is this seat taken?" a male voice asks and despite my prowl I am quite annoyed to be approached so soon in my hunt.

"No, but there are plenty of couches in the lobby. Must you sit right next to the only person occupying a seat?" I look at him and there is a vague familiarity, but he could've been anyone. If he frequented the hotel at all in the last few years, I could have seen him before. Either way, he was not put off by my disapproval of his company.

"You look familiar," he said rehearsed as if he'd worked up his nerves before sitting down.

I could tell he was holding his breath for my response. He was handsome though in a haven't-slept-in-months kind of way. Clean but tired and likely well into a few drinks. It was just after one pm.

"Come here often?" I roll my eyes, uncross then re-cross my legs in the opposite direction. He is taking the fun out of finding a fling. Further, he is far too interested and even more familiar for my comfort.

"Ummm. Can I..?" he started.

I stand, take down over half a glass of wine in one fell gulp and turn to leave.

"Wait, please." He stands up slower than his plead for me to stay. His demeanor changes as he uses his hand to smooth his shirt. He clears his throat and regains his footing before continuing. "I wanted to ask you to dinner."

"Tomorrow night. Seven pm. Meet me here."

I leave him standing there with what little dignity he managed to pull out at the last moment. It saved him. Had he continued to act like a spineless punk, I would not have agreed. Yet, everything inside of me screams in protest. Maybe I have seen him before, but if I had, I need to know for sure and from where.

I pick a sexy form-fitting black cocktail dress and show up an hour early hoping to catch Malcom before his shift is over, but some new bartender is chatting up an elderly couple in matching denim seated at the bar.

"You must, be Sylvia!" he climes loudly as I sit down.

My facial expression is fixed and I show neither affirmation nor objection.

"And this must be your chardonnay. Malcom told me to expect you."

"He must have also told you how much I hate small talk."

"He did," the gentleman deflates himself and returns to the couple.

Inside I am screaming with red flags. I should leave. Chicken out. But would he come back here looking for me? This is seriously the only thing I do to pass the time. Maybe he won't show up. I should have caught his name and simply looked him up like any other overly cautious dating woman would.

After a while and one glass down, I find a bit of courage and hail the bartender for another. Glancing up at the clock above the bar, I turn my chair to face the main doors. He still has a few minutes. Surely he wouldn't keep a lady waiting.

There he is. My heart in my throat at the reality slowly sinking in. I imagine this was what it feels like when your husband catches you cheating. I am frozen and all blood leaves my face cold. I should run. I should throw up. It is not the young man who asked me to dinner the night before, but a face I know better than my own. The man I dream of every night. The only man I've ever wanted but could never have is staring at me from across the room. He knows me. I am the reason he's there. John Smith.

He pushes from the pillar and moves toward me. I want this to end with me in his arms, but I know it won't. He's not real. The young man from the day before knew who I was when he sat down. John is not a real person. I designed him down to the pattern of his facial hair, yet he is getting closer. He knows my secret and who I am. There will be no running. I have to kill him and this is my only chance at getting him first.

"Hello, John," flirting. I fight my voice not to quiver. Such a dirty trick to play on a girl.

"Sylvia." He tips his head to me like an old friend, and I melt inside like a school girl. My breath is caught in the dryness of my throat. I take a long drink of wine.

"So, you're a thief? Stealing a lady's things." I wish I had poison to slip into his double scotch.

"Good guess but no. Took me years to duplicate your programming. Even in the minutes you were in that room I memorized your alias' face. What I thought was your face. Once I figured he was a cover, took me no time to track you down."

A job. He had been a job. How did he know?

"Then you must be CIA. They gave me a contract on an agent. Guess we have similar luck." Then it his face comes back to me. San Diego. His wife was the mark. Now I know I am not making it out of this lobby.

"Her name was Grace. We found out that morning she was five weeks pregnant. My daughter would be three years old now." He does not break eye contact. "I wanted you to know that before you die."

John and his deep smooth voice. If anyone were to deliver me to my end, it would be the crystal blue eyes of the man I loved. He keeps his gaze even as a tear falls from my cheek and onto my hand.

I look down at my glass. No taste, and went down easy. He planted it before I came in. The bartender meets my gaze, knowingly. His guy. My head is getting heavier and my throat is tight. I can't really hear anything but the rapid pounding of my pulse.

If this is my end, I am content to die in front of him. He is not my John Smith, but he'll do. I reach up with what I know is the last of my strength. I touch his face and put my lips to his.

I was the only one I ever loved.

The Last Piece

Soon after starting my first novel, I got stuck. I researched ways to work through blocks and stumbled on the suggestion of working on something else. This began my journey in writing short fiction. "The Last Piece" is my first short story as an adult writer. Note: Grab some tissues and proceed with caution.

If there were ever a perfect place, this is where it would be. The roar of the water would drown out her crying. The search parties had moved through the area already and focused their efforts downstream days ago. It was here where he was last seen on his school field trip. Her baby was lost. The park rangers assumed he fell through the railing into the rushing waters of the creek that ran through the national forest. It was day three. The sky was turning orange. She had not slept, showered, or eaten at all.

Jessica sat down on the wooden path that ran the height of the waterfall with landings and stairs climbing up, up, up to the top. She felt her feet swell upon relieving them of the pressure of standing. She slipped her back pack off, unzipped it, and pulled out a flag folded into a triangle, a picture frame, a notebook, a pen, a lantern, and a bottle of wine arranging them neatly. She also set aside her coat and a pillow with a cartoon Iron Man where his little head had lay.

The picture was of her, her late husband, and their one and only son three years ago. Her knee length sundress was yellow and white. Her sunglasses hid her puffy eyes and lack of makeup. Jake was only five and knew his daddy was going to fly helicopters in the desert. He knew about good guys and bad guys, but none of them knew this would be the last time they would all be together. Hank's Blackhawk was shot down. He had not survived. If it were not for Jake, Jessica Warren would not have survived either.

She uncorked the wine. The label was elaborate with her and Hank's initials in black and red, saved from their wedding nearly a decade ago. Silent tears streaked her cheeks as she took a long drink from the bottle. She could not taste it for grief had dulled all her senses. She took a deep breath and looked up at the sky. Blue faded to orange clouds above her. She remembered the camera she had given Jake for their first Christmas after losing Hank. She told him, it was a way for him to show his daddy how he sees the world. Every year after, she printed a book of the pictures for his dad, a coping mechanism.

Jessica had her own coping mechanism: her writing. She wrote Hank letters like he was still in the desert waiting for his time to be up so he could come home. Now she would write letters to her baby boy, forever on a field trip to the national forest. The hole in her heart suddenly felt like it would swallow her. It shook her soul, and with her tears came a scream so loud the roar of the waterfall was no match. She pulled the pillow into her and squeezed it so close to her body. She buried her face so hard it hurt, trying to smell him, trying to hold him one last time. For hours she sat like this, rocking back and forth, cycling through various intensities of sobs.

The sky was black and the air began to chill. She set the pillow neatly down and wrapped herself in her coat. She turned on the lantern and remembered how she would use it during thunderstorms to keep Jake from being too scared. He was everywhere. There was not one thing in this world that would not bring him back to her mind, ripping her apart over and over again. She took another long drink from the bottle and picked up the pen, wiping her tears with the back of her hand so she could see what was going on the paper.

My sweet little boy Jake,

Where did you go, baby? Where are you? I've looked and looked. My heart has searched for you in this wilderness but I still can't find you. You took a piece of me with you. It was the last piece, and Mommy needs it back. Mommy needs you to come back. I promise you're not in trouble. I promise I will never let you go. I promise that I will hold you forever and never let you go. I promise that you will never go another day without receiving every ounce of love I can give you.

Jakey, Mommy can't do this without you. You're the man of the house. Who is going to protect me? Who is going to hold me and let me tell stories about your daddy?

Jacob Henry Warren, I love you with every part of my soul. I cannot go on in a world without you or your daddy. I don't know where I will go, but I hope it's a place where we can be a family again. But if it's not, then I hope you find

your daddy and he picks up where I had to let go.
I will always love you my sweet son.

Love, Mommy.

Jessica's tears dropped on the paper, smearing the fresh ink. She reached again for her bag. The bottle rattled as her hand searched blindly until it met her fingers. Lithium had been the only thing to get her through Hank's death and kept her functioning and healthy so she could care for her son alone. It would help again today. She had refilled her prescription just the day before Jake's disappearance. She poured the bottle's contents into her hand which threatened to overflow. She emptied her cupped hand into her mouth and followed it with the bottle of wine. Three. Deep. Drinks.

She laid her head on the pillow when the bush beside her rustled. She prayed it was an animal come to maul her to death. Though her vision blurred, she could still make out the red t-shirt, and the little body wearing it.

"Mommy? Mommy! I found you!"

Nonfiction

Nonfiction is called many things: memoirs, essays, journals. To me, nonfiction is most entertaining when we take the form of a life story verbally told and translate the same tone and emotion into writing.

Creative nonfiction adopts the literary techniques often found in fiction, but tells a true story, while essays are a journey of thought not focusing on one particular scene or event. Most people begin their writing journey with keeping personal journals. I am no exception, though you will not find those entries here. I welcome you to take a step inside my train (pun intended) of thought.

Writing a World

I like to keep my goals in written common places around the house - my bathroom mirror, my planner, on the wall in front of my face when I fall asleep and wake up every day, etc. This book is one of those goals which will push me closer to those bigger goals. I find this passage fitting as an opener for my collection of writings. Someone could argue this as fiction, but in my heart this scene exists in my journey of life. Today and tomorrow do not hold the following moment hostage.

I write in the wee morning light when everything slumbers and the day is merely a pink-orange glow. The night animals tuck into their dark spaces to escape the light, and the day creatures roll sleepily from where they claimed as a home the night before. My children are snuggled up so warm and peaceful. Pups sleep at the foot of our bed still warming my husband's feet. Crickets have stopped and birds have not started. This is the silence which tickles my muse to awaken.

My wooden desk sits slightly shorter than most. It's perfect for me. The old and worn wood is soft; generations of pen wielding arms pulled from left to right creating hand written letters, stories, and poems have rounded front ledge. Parchment replaced by technology: a double screen, wireless keyboard and mouse. The sentiment remains the same. These distract slightly from the vintage of the scene, but are a necessity in the production of my craft.

My chair sometimes requires a conscious balance. Leaning back is a guaranteed concussion, but the arm rests serve their purpose. The cushion needed reupholstering when my grandmother was a child. The red, orange, and yellow fibers are still vibrant nearest the wooden frame, but the seat has a comfortable divot to accommodate my posture. Nothing comes close to this custom fit. I have purchased new chairs, but none offer the history and familiarity of this heirloom.

My coffee sits to the left of my keyboard. Its steam carries the aroma of emerging clarity. The scent brings me from the fog of sleep into the world I have created on the screen. Sometimes the two intertwine in my dreams. Other times I require the liquid motivation to bring me back to the place where my journey started, like a conditional learning pattern. I keep a black pen near my journal on the right. The journal, composed of recycled material, has rough, beige pages. My pen spills more ink than needed making my thoughts appear bold and important against the imperfect paper.

A picture frame proudly displays a collage of my family: two happy adults with their silly and adorable son and daughter. Two beagles are never far from the subjects. A calendar sits between the two large screens for literary reference and sometimes to remind me of where I am in time, if ever I get lost.

WRITING A WORLD

I hide all clocks and measures of minute time. My children are my alarm in this place. I have reached a state where they no longer compete for my attention. My work is completed in the morning's silence, not in the corporate bustle of obligation. When they rise, I save my work for a later time when I am not actively called Mom. When bellies are full and heads are resting. This is when I find this desk, my old friend.

The nook of my space extends the living room, pushed against the wall underneath a wide window. It faces south, so the sun passes by as it makes its daily journey but never looks directly in. With the pane cracked even just an inch, the sound of the rushing creek engulfs me in a whirl, both strong and gentle. The rushing water ushers a breeze which carries the aroma of the over-hanging willow and tall standing oaks accompanied by mellow sassafras. The circulation of earth and coffee transport me to the place where my thoughts become those of someone else. Where primal fears fuel the adrenaline needed for survival. Where lust is mistaken for love. Where death is not the end once perceived to be. The world is no longer confined to what is tangible, but is anything I can articulate.

Sometimes, I do not even write. Sometimes I hold my coffee with two hands, lean carefully back in my soft and unstable chair and I search. My mind steps out of the window and floats amongst the leaves of the trees, falling to the water to chase the rapids between rocks. I think of other places and who I might find there. I put them in situations and create their reactions. I allow myself to feel emotions that belong to others and make a note of their progression.

With sounds behind me, a giggle, a yawn, sometimes even a flush, I am brought back to the world I cherish above any other I could imagine. Where my calendar reminds me of how far I have come and the little people so excited for the day they woke up and are that much older. They look forward to the real adventure Mommy will take them on, for the journey they will live and the emotions of situations that are their own.

Before leaving, I glance one more time at my space and thank God for the gift and the ability to give to my children what I had only dreamed of.

Little Mary Magdalene

My grandmother, Ms. Mary Magdalene Gilliam (Werner), was a true matriarch in the most humble and meek sense. She never talked about herself or told stories about growing up in Kansas in the 1930s and 40s. She loved a good Christian romance novel, but was never a storyteller herself. Strangely, she produced many subsequent storytellers, writers, and authors in her children and grandchildren. The earliest and only story I heard about my family history was more about my Great-Grandmother, Regina Philomena Werner (Schmidt). My grandmother told this story to her daughter, Jacqueline, who shared it with me.

It was a rare and likely less serious occasion if Regina Werner spanked a one of her ten living children.

"No," she insisted. "If you really want to teach a child a lesson, you sit them down and really teach them."

Not sparing a swat for missed manners or a grounding for

breaking the rules, if one of her children really messed up, she sat them down on a tall, four legged wood stool—the one missing the foot bars so their feet just dangled uncomfortably—and lectured them for hours on end depending on the chore she completed while the child watched and listened. The older children caught on quick, but the little ones still had much to learn. They often begged for spankings just to be done with the offense.

Mary was called a baby, though Tony and Rudy were the babies. As the youngest and markedly petite girl, Mary wanted to measure up to her older brothers and sisters. She decided one day to approach her mama, Regina, and request a chore out in the farm.

"Mama, I wanna help, too." Her pigtails swung back and forth, grazing her full cheeks. Mary crossed her arms and stretched her height. "I'm big. I can help Johnny feed cows, or Teresa collect eggs."

"Little Mary Magdalene," Regina sighed over a full sink of dishes. "You dropped the eggs last time she let you help, honey."

"Mama, I can do something."

Regina paused and looked out the window over the hills of their Kansas farm. A smile spread on her face. She stepped away from the dishes, drying her hands on her apron and lowered herself level with Little Mary.

"I've got just the thing for you, tiny one," she said smiling and touching a finger to her daughter's nose. "There's a storm on the horizon. Go out, collect all the baby chicks, and shut them in the coop so they don't get blown away by the winds."

Pride and resolve settled in the preschooler's shoulders.

"Yes, Mama."

Little Mary, head high, marched to the yard where the chicken coop sat open near the pond. Tiny birds cheeped while other larger ones quacked, but both kinds were cute and fuzzy with their baby bird down and no real feathers. Mary herded the quick little baby birds into the coop with nothing short of a hard time because the small wooden house was full to the brim. Somehow, Little Mary on her tip-toes latched that coop door before the very first drop of rain splashed her youthful cheek.

The next morning, Teresa burst into kitchen from the back door, hysterical and ignoring the mud caked on her boots as she smudged by the little ones eating breakfast.

"Oh Mama, all the chicks!" was all the blubbering girl could muster with an arm full of chirpless balls of down. "There were ducklings in the coop, Mama. They crushed all the chicks, but one. Who even puts ducks in a coop, Mama? What a mean thing to do!"

Regina knew and sighed heavily, "Teresa, get your damned boots out of my kitchen and get these out of the house! Then come back and sweep up all the mess you tracked in. You know better than this."

Mary stopped chewing her toast, her mouth far too dry to even attempt to swallow. Before she could stop them, tears spilled over her cheeks. The ball in her throat caught crumbs on an inhale, sending the half chewed bread flying across the table in a fit of coughing.

Regina just watched the tot through coughs, gasps, and sobs waiting for the little one to calm down.

"Come on, Little Mary Magdalene. Sit here on this stool." Regina Warner proceeded to give her daughter such a detailed lecture on the visual differences between ducks and chicks, the importance of hatching, growing, and selling chickens for their livelihood and a definitive, nonnegotiable timeframe of when Mary could try her hand at helping again.

This lecture stayed with Little Mary Magdalene through her teenage years, and into adulthood. The lecture stayed with her through raising her own children, them having children, and through Mary having great-grandchildren. In fact, this singular lecture at age four was the only specific story she ever shared to anyone about her childhood.

Baghdad ER

From October 2007 to January 2009, I was deployed for the first time to Baghdad, where I worked as a medic in the Emergency Room of Sadam's former hospital, Ibn Sina. Though I had four years of army experience then, I was only twenty-two when I arrived and twenty-four when I returned. While others, like our head doctor Todd Baker, chose to reflect on the experience immediately, I waited over a decade to look back at my experience in the busiest trauma center in the world. The lack of punctuation in sections of this narrative signify a stream of consciousness of the main character. I assure you, this story is fully edited and those omissions are intentional.

"Gilliam! Take thirty minutes and go clean up," her shift leader commanded.

Karen was dismissed from her shift after only working three of her twelve hours. She had not bothered to look down at herself since the first combat casualty rolled in missing both legs and another whose left side of her body clung to limbs by thin white threads of tendons and ligaments. Karen's digital patterned army uniform was saturated with blood not her own. Her hands were clean, though, up to her wrists.

She walked out the door into the night instead of taking the shortcut through the well-lit air-conditioned hallways of the Iraqi hospital. She stopped at the gazebo where four benches faced inward at a large metal bucket filled with sand. It was midnight, and empty for the moment.

The sound of her Velcro pocket was muffled by the adrenaline still pumping through her body. She pulled out a pack of American branded cigarettes, dry and fragile from the desert climate. A brisk wind blew at her exposed neck, drying the sweat and blood and giving her a chill as she lit the end and took two long drags.

She stared. In the night, she looked at an object a thousand miles away in silence. Her mind blank but also running as fast as her heart was beating.

Her body was still, but her mind ran backward until she was standing at the head of the bed of a soldier, talking to him because he so desperately wanted to sleep but Karen knew if he fell asleep too soon they would lose him.

What's your name where are you from do you have someone special back home? Well, we're gonna get you back there just hold tight and look at me focus on me listen to my voice. Wow, you have some very nice eyes young man, just hold on a bit longer we're going to take care of you. No water for you buddy we are going to get you up to surgery stay with me the doctor is coming over in just a second just hold on until the doctor gets here. You look worse off than I will ever let you know man. I have no idea if you're going to make it but I will say everything I possibly can to keep your blood pressure in check for just a few more minutes.

Then you can go to sleep while a machine breathes for you and they do their best to save your life in the operating room. Are you binge-watching anything cool at the moment? Oh, I've never seen that but hang on, I'm gonna move to the side and let the doctor talk to you okay, I'm right here just answer the doctor's questions and well get you upstairs. I'm telling you small white lies because once you are intubated, I have to leave you and go to the next guy that is probably going to lose his hand. I'll continue this rotation, one after another until you are all out of the emergency room and what was once organized chaos, turns to quiet. When I can sit down and think about everything I just witnessed and your blood dries stiff on my uniform.

Michael did have some handsome blue eyes. Later, she would ask for the survival rate of the mass casualty event which took up only the first part of her shift, but she would not ask for who, if any, did not make it. If Michael were among the lost, Karen would have lied to a dead man. At 23 years-old, looking into his eyes and telling him he was fine would make a long life with a mistake she couldn't make right. 98% was the average survival rate, but even that percentage meant that by the end of the fifteen-month deployment, 150 US soldiers would come into her emergency room and not make it out.

Cleaned with the contaminated uniform and boots stuffed into a bag, she plastered her hair to her head with product and secured the rest into a tight bun on the back of her head. A small amount of makeup powder sent to her in a care package from home hid the permanent dark circles under her eyes. She opened the glass door to her balcony and sat in silence, lighting another cigarette. This was against the rules, but just below her the hospital incinerator blew smoke up the side of the four-story apartment building in which her unit lived. They might not die on the battlefield, but in thirty years, most of them would probably pass from lung cancer, smokers and nonsmokers alike.

Smoking was not allowed on the balcony, not because it was inconsiderate to her neighbors or a fire hazard, but because it made her a sniper target. High about the tall Texas concrete barriers, the city of Baghdad was black but for a few street lights. Windows of buildings had been painted, so even though the lights were on in her room, the bright red cherry light of her cigarette was an easy target in the otherwise black night.

Most attacks were not small arms fire. They were rockets. Ten months into the deployment and explosions lost their novelty. One's mortality was already determined. If a missile hit wherever you were at the time, it was just meant to be. Nothing you could have done differently. Walk, run. Go left or right. Stay in bed or take cover. The sirens detecting the incoming bombs would sound and most would look at one another, take one more drag from their cigarette and wait to hear where the first one landed. If the impact were a distance away, they would make their way back into the building. If the first bomb were close by, they would drop to the ground and wait for the next before running for their lives into a nearby bunker.

She continued her smoke, looking across the street to the once regal government building. Now a giant hole exposed the gold lined stair cases and elaborately designed marble interior. In the daylight, she could see all five floors of marble-tiled floors and the exposed extravagant dome of the internal ceiling. The pools and palm trees still left a ghost of an impression that Baghdad was once a beautiful metropolis which functioned just like the capital of her own home.

These people want freedom, they want safety, they want to go back to the way things were before women and children were murdered by the hundreds with chemical warfare. Could it ever be again the home that these people were forced out of? There are so many children still left within the city while just south the smoke still rose from the liberation of the terrorist sect in Sadar City. Fires had been burning for days. The hospital staff even took casualties from that fight as the rebellions thought little of the Geneva Convention. How do we fight an enemy that has no rules and looks like everyone else? They sacrifice their own children as acceptable collateral damage. She'd seen it. A little boy sat quietly on a gurney in the hallway. He sat upright with his knees bent and his intestines poked out of a gash in his belly. He was not critical, but that poor little boy was alone.

Would he ever get back to his family or would he even survive after he left would he succumb to infection where are his parents? Would the hospital staff even do anything to locate them or anyone in the boy's family or would they just drop them off at the gates of the mythical Iraqi Med City where thousands of local nationals die before receiving appropriate care? Do they care?

The dry tobacco burnt so fast, the cigarette went out before she'd noticed. She collected the soiled garments and took them down to in the incinerator to be burned with the rest of the medical waste. Her sleeve caught on something sharp inside of a red bag. She winced and pulled free. She'd bandage her scratch when she got back to the ER, but she could hear the inbound Blackhawks approaching and made her way to treat the next set of casualties.

War and Coffee

For me, war and coffee go hand in hand. I simply cannot have one without thinking of the other.

"Dacia, do you mean war figuratively?"

No, I mean war in the very literal sense of the word. More specifically, coffee reminds me of the war on terrorism and Iraq.

Before I get too far ahead of myself, let me add that I have always loved the smell of coffee. My dad's parents both drank it constantly throughout their day. The smell of coffee and cigarettes was a staple of childhood. Strangely enough I did not learn how to drink coffee until well into my twenties. I find myself, even today, modifying the potion with the latest trend in sweeteners. The nostalgia it brings now does not take me back to my grandparent's small house in Henderson, Kentucky. It takes me to a place of horror and self-discovery; of trauma and triumph.

War smells like dirt and raw chicken. Baghdad circa 2007 through 2009; I worked in the emergency room in the "Green Zone", also known as Baghdad ER. It was more secure than most places per square foot, however it was still dangerous. Rarely were we shot at with simple gunfire, but often we stood under threat of mortars and rockets that targeted the hospital compound daily. At that point, it was luck of the draw if you lived or not. Lucky for me and the entire hospital staff, we had no fatalities due to enemy fire power. You may think of this as a successful mission, but roughly over 150 young men and women that call USA home did not come out of that ER in the fifteen months I worked there. We still maintained a 98% survival rate despite this. You can do the math. I've seen a lot of trauma.

"Coffee, Dacia. Bring it back to coffee."

There was an abundance of Starbucks coffee donated to the hospital by various well-wishers, family members, and strangers wanting nothing more than to support their troops. There was so much coffee, and everyone drank so much coffee. This is where my coffee journey actually began. I started to mix hot chocolate in with hot coffee with random creamers only for the simple fact that I was exhausted and had little options for energy otherwise. I had no idea what I was doing. Then one day I staked my claim on one of the ceramic mugs in the kitchen. It was mine. Everyone knew: this is Dacia's coffee mug. I became brave, and figured out how to go without the sweet hot chocolate mix. The recipe for Dacia's coffee was 4 little creamer cups and 6 packets of sugar. This remained the standard for my remaining time in the third world country.

Coffee and cigarettes. We called it a Boston Breakfast. In the heat of a mass casualty situation, I remember walking swiftly passed the nurses' station with my buddy holding up my mug. With a quick thank you, I grabbed it and drank as much as I could on my errand to retrieve supplies or relay a message before making my way back into the trauma bay. Many times, in the middle of the night when the last patient made it up to the operating room, the morgue, or wherever they were headed, we would sit in the gazebo and just stare off a million miles into nothing, smoking and sipping. Occasional statements were met with a mumble of agreement, without making eye contact. In the winter we wouldn't shiver while we sat outside; only if our sweat began to catch the cold, steam rising from our mugs and the backs of our shirts. Ultimately, coffee meant it was over. We had time to stop and smell the coffee as there aren't many flowers in the desert. It meant that we made it, even though others did not. It also meant that we could regroup before the next disaster made its way into our care.

I carry this with me now. PTSD triggered by coffee. I still prefer ceramic mugs to travel ones, with thick handles that hold the highest setting on the Keurig. Sipping coffee is motivating. Yes, you can attribute it to the caffeine and that is fine; but for me, it means that I have strength left to finish the mission. My missions lately are nothing to what they were nine years ago. I still work in a hospital, but it sits on American soil and my coffee and I are tucked safely behind a desk and in an office. I love coffee like I love that fifteen month stay in Iraq. It was horrible and nasty and was way too hot, but with the right recipe it was tolerable.

Life On The Extra Board

Much like military family life, the railroad has many challenges. A common struggle is being on call 24/7 and the effect not having a set schedule of constant travel has on a family. There is no easy way to explain to people why I always anticipate my husband being gone on weekends, holidays, and special occasions. Wives of railroaders seek each other out for solidarity and this is my ode to them.

Twelve hours drug on like a lame dog. Red lights had the train stopped with the view of a cow pasture to the left and a highway on the right - the middle of nowhere. Two hours into the trip and dispatch had the train stopped in a siding to let another train, likely hauling the mail, run around. With no one else but the engineer for ten hours of the day, the conductor stared out the window, nodding off every now and again. The next day was his son's fourth birthday, but at a standstill there was little chance he would make it home before the little tike went to bed.

He had only seen his daughter roll over for the first time from a recording his wife sent. Tapping his knee anxiously, he waited for the green light. Instead, the two men sat on the motionless train waiting for a van to deliver their relief and transport them to their destination: a dirty hotel in a small town surrounded by the Great Plains without consistent wifi. Bored and tired, he was ready for the day to be over. A video call with his son would have to do. He missed his wife, his two kids, their dogs, but knew the sacrifice of being away was only temporary and worth giving his family everything.

Twelve hours came like a slap to the face. The railroader's wife could use a few more hours in the day. With two little one's tummies full, her dinner was cold as usual. The baby chatted in her high chair while she packed the dishwasher and ate. The boy played with toys on the floor. With bottles washed and bags packed for the next day, she ran down a mental list of things left to do to prepare for another solo go at parenting. Her own lunch prepared to grab for the morning, she took a few more minutes to clean up the living room before she scooped up the baby and carried dirty clothes with her upstairs.

Then baths, PJs, teeth brushed, stories told, milk refilled, bedtime snack given. She cuddled the babe back to sleep, offered more milk to the boy pleading for him to stay in his bed. Finally, she took her shoes and work clothes off.

The next day was her son's birthday, and she had to wake up early to bake his cake before work. The mother collapsed onto her bed, which was far too big for one person, and moved to his side to find his scent still on his pillow. A deep breath reminded her she could do this. He did not leave them because he wanted to, but so they could live comfortably and give their children everything they ever wanted. TV served as a nightlight while she went through photos on her phone, deleting what she could spare to make room for the ones she needed to take for her husband the next day. Exhausted, she hardly made it to 9pm.

12am a little boy appeared. Too tired to fight, she let him snuggle until she woke up enough to return him to bed. 2am, a sleepy baby girl cried for milk. Twenty minutes to satisfy her hunger then back to bed. She glanced at the clock. 3 more hours until her alarm went off and no idea what day of the week it was. She missed her husband, but understood her sacrifice was only temporary and worth giving their family everything.

Mom-Clique

I am quite a gregarious introvert with a large fear of missing out, or what the kids call Fo-Mo. Fo-Mo keeps most people scrolling through social media at all hours of the night. I might have to wake-up at 5 a.m., but Susan's love life is like an episode of The Young and the Restless. I cannot turn away. This week her partner is Joslyn, a grocery clerk at the organic store. Jonathan has been completely wiped clean of her FaceBook photo albums as if he never existed three days ago. My head is spinning. If I got out more, maybe my life would be more exciting. Catch me at kindergarten drop off or the grocery store, I am quick with a joke, but you'll likely not see me elsewhere.

Having moved every three years since I was born, I don't typically keep friends close. Meaning I know from their social media the major highlights of life, but lack the intimate knowledge of how they're really doing. At the same time I try to post on social media regularly so as to minimize the need for anyone to personally see how I'm doing. Not that I would stiff arm anyone who approached me. It's just exhausting to me to keep up constant interaction.

In 2014 my husband and I purchased our forever home, digging in roots I have no experience in growing. Our first winter in the house, my neighbor across the street invited my family over for her annual Christmas Eve house party. I said yes in a moment of outgoing energy but as my introverted brain took over, I seriously had no intention of attending.

The day of, I weighed some pros and cons. Pros: 1. I told her we would be there. 2. There would be other people with kids there. 3. I needed to get out of the house for something other than work and if I walked straight out my front door, I'd be standing on her porch so there was no real excuse not to go. Cons: I don't wanna. What if I said something stupid?

My husband, kids and I walked across the street that Christmas Eve and enjoyed ourselves. Beth and I had kids around the same age who played nicely together.

"The neighborhood's social media group is really in everyone's business," was the only relatable topic I could come up with.

"Apparently people post pictures of a child swing sets with an address to advertise swinger parties," another person chimed. "Someone in the playdate group was going on about it."

"Oh no," Jaime laughed as she bounced her infant son on her knee. "It's the houses with the business cards under a large rock in the front yard. That's how you really know who the swingers are."

I finished my almost full glass of wine. Is that what this party was? A swinger's audition? Should I look outside under rocks for business cards? I'll admit I love a good drama. I just don't love being in the good drama. From then on, I kept an ear on every conversation in the room, but heard no propositions of extramarital sex. Thank God.

Over the following months I discovered Darci, Kayla, Kristen and Beth were basically a mom-clique. They posted fun pictures of their nights out wine tasting with their prefect smiling faces and I secretly wished to be invited. Again, with no real intention to go. Just being invited would be so cool. Like having real friends who may or may not want to sleep with my husband. I was hoping they didn't, but I still had my reservations.

Christmas Eve rolled around again, but this time I looked forward to it. I picked out a dress and prepared some food. I stalked the attendees I met briefly the year before as to not embarrassingly reintroduce myself for the second time. As the night progressed, I noticed a marked absence. Beth and her family did not come. And I knew they were in town because of the adorable matching pajama pictures posted that morning on their living room stairs.

"So, Beth doesn't like us anymore," Darci explained. "Yeah, she went psycho and deleted all of us from Facebook. She probably deleted you, too."

This shot up a red flags with me because Beth is still friends with me on Facebook, which means not only did she unfriend all of her friends but she blocked them, too.

So, for no particular reason to mention, I got completely smashed. Not like white-girl wasted but black out drunk. I was so embarrassed not having a recollection of the end of the night. I passed out (at home luckily) and Greg managed stage our children's Christmas gifts himself. I will never drink again (a lie).

A few weeks later I bumped into Kristen at yoga and she completely ignored me. I must have embarrassed myself in the worst way. I texted Darci because she's blunt and who I felt was the ring leader of this gang.

Me (texting): *Do you have a second for an honest answer?*
Waiting and waiting and waiting... This can't be good.

Darci: *Sure. What's up?*

Me: *On a scale of 1-10, how bad was I on Christmas?*

Darci: *10 being horrible?*

Oh My F-ing God I KNEW IT!!! Heat and a little vomit crept up my throat. Three little dots on my cell phone screen winked me in the face for what felt like an eternity.

Darci: *Totally a 1. You were so much fun! We'd love to hang out with you again sometime.*

What?!?! The clique wanted to hang out with ME? I mean I know I'm pretty stinking cool, but they thought so, too?

A few weeks later I was added to a group text. Then came the invite for Lemon Drop Cocktails on a school night. How can I say no?! I skipped—100% accurate description—across the street that night and was officially christened into the mom-clique with a matching group coffee (wine) mug. And while I always fantasized as the writer of the group I would be the Carrie, I am indeed the prude and proper Charlotte. And, thankfully, no ever asked to sleep with me or my husband.

Now what??? I continue to navigate having multiple friends and instead of living vicariously through their exciting lives online, I satisfy my Fo-Mo by being a part of them. Down the road, if they un-friend me, my inner introvert will likely throw a party of one. Until then, I get to post pictures of multiple smiling faces with delicious cocktails for others to admire at 2 a.m. wondering why Beth was completely wiped clean of our FaceBook photo albums as if she never existed three days ago.

Poetry

My weakest talent in writing rests in the prosy flows of poetry. All but one of these pieces were written before I ever considered myself a writer, and only then because I was forced to. One of these things is not like the other and it will not be hard to spot the transition in talent.

There was a time when I found it easy to write poetry. When my adolescent and young adult demons were well fed and I struggled to find myself. Once, my husband and I went through our basement and years of boxes we have packed around our entire adult lives from houses, cities, states, and failed relationships. I stumbled upon letters from my father, letters from my husband when we were deployed to two different countries, and old poems I had written many lifetimes ago. I have no recollection of the context of this poem, but goodness I was in a horrible place.

Sorrow is usually the common muse of poetry and memory lane brings sad poems of a young girl struggling to fit in, find love, and to love herself.

Showcase

I hate the way you love me
The way you feed on my misery
Thirsting for my tears and sweat that fall
    to the ground,
Watering the garden of your ego
I am your accessory
I smile for your convenience
Standing on a pedestal you placed me on
    to drink freely
On the attention from other men.
I cannot leave you.
You have taken all from me.
I cannot breathe without you.
Yet when you sleep, I am alone again.
You hurt me when you tore down my walls
I cry when you touch me.
I kept you at arm's length, but you still
    broke through.
It's not okay. I'm not okay.

What you have taken from me, I can never give again.
But still you ask for more... more...
I only have but one soul.
Now I am a ghost who sleeps in your bed
A memory of who I used to be and who you tell people I am.

Masterpiece

Erase me from this painting of chaos
If you can find me
I seem to fit in so well
Captive of my own choices
Pride and lust are my brushes
I paint with colors of shame and regret
Mistakes soil the canvas
Merely a fruitless struggle to become myself
Trapped by loaded words and accusations
But only the walls hear my silent screams...
This is my Masterpiece...

Don't You Know

For Jude and Val

Don't you know that you are mine
That I will carry, and feed and warm
That I will always see and watch you
Don't you know that you are mine

Don't you know how small you are
That I will fight and worry and love
That I will suffer and hurt before I let
    you
Don't you know how small you are

Don't you know that you have me
That I will fear and cherish and cry
That I will wait for the call from you
Don't you know you have me

Plays

As a novelist, I do not have a particular opinion or insight about writing plays aside from the literary form being far from my favorite. I do not play to adapt by books to films when they get optioned. Plenty of professionals get paid good money to do such things.

Both plays to follow were class assignments. I worked incredibly hard on them and figured I would share this hard work with the world. I have included these at the end for anyone who strong armed their way through this entire book. Thank you Mom.

Is The Mind Not Of The Body?

In studying the later Victorian Era and writers such as Oscar Wilde and the ceaseless traveler Robert Louis Stevenson, I was tasked with exploring the perpetual identity crisis of the time. When "Being Ernest" was actually dishonest and Mr. Hyde was indeed Dr. Jekyll, writers also found themselves hiding their true selves as in the tragic case of Mr. Wilde.

I enjoy flexing my creativity in ways that are not typical of my normal fiction writing. This lends itself well to becoming a well-rounded writer and an author unbound by genre. This is another historical piece with twists and turns.

Characters

>DOCTOR HANK CHARLESTON, a psychotherapist in his late 50s

>CHARLIE HENDERSON, a troubled man and subject of HANK's psychoanalysis

Setting

In DOCTOR CHARLESTON's office, early 1900 Europe

At rise, CHARLIE is seated in a chair across from HANK, sitting identically across from him. The two are separated by a wall but visible to each other through what appears to the audience as an open threshold.

HANK: Good morning, sir. Let's start by introducing ourselves. This is an easy enough practice. I am Doctor Hank Charleston, as I am sure your caretakers have informed you. Please, tell me who you are.

CHARLIE: I am Ernest.

HANK: You are earnest as in honest, or you prefer the name Ernest?

CHARLIE: It's not up for interpretation. It is what it is. I am Ernest.

HANK: Fair enough, Ernest. From where do you hail?

CHARLIE: I am from nowhere. I've stayed mobile through my days and claim no place as my home.

HANK: Alright, from where do your parents hail?

(Both men shift in their seat)

CHARLIE: They reside in Edinburgh, where I was born. But I am not from there. I take pieces of places that I travel and carry them with me in spirit. I visit France, and gain a French accent. I travel to New York and develop short patience. My influences stay fluid.

IS THE MIND NOT OF THE BODY?

HANK: Do you understand why you are here today?

CHARLIE: I am ill in body.

HANK: Ah, you see I am a doctor of the mind.

CHARLIE: The mind is of the body, good doctor. I assure you I am not crazy.

HANK: Are you of nobility or of poverty?

CHARLIE: I am of that which I am. If I appear rich to you, then am I not a rich man? If I appear a pauper, do I not have any worth? My social standing has little to do with the weight of my purse.

HANK: You would appear to me as a man of indecision, Mr. Henderson.

CHARLIE: I am Ernest.

HANK: Pardon me, Ernest. I can see already that my agenda means little to you in the ways of treatment. What is it you wish me to do for you that I cannot decide by my observations?

CHARLIE: I wish for you to look away from what is in front of you. By looking too deep into a subject, one will draw their very own conclusions which would be contrary to that of its true intention.

HANK: What is your true intention, might I ask? If assumedly one is wrong, how then can one know the true meaning if not told outright?

CHARLIE: It is no concern the true meaning that is simply the point. Let be and it holds its place where it belongs.

HANK: Where *you* belong.

CHARLIE: I am Ernest.

HANK: I am beginning to think that your claim to honesty and earnestness is simply a diversion to a lie you wish me to believe.

CHARLIE: Who is lying to whom, doctor? I tell you of my life and you tell me it is a lie? One that would not know me from the next fellow would tell me where I am from and what I am called.

HANK: In my profession, I am accustomed to one attempting to mislead me into thinking they are one way, when indeed they are quite the opposite. You tell me are Ernest, but you leave little evidence to a namesake or a state of moral being of that which you claim. I ask what you would have me believe and you talk around the answer, attempting to divert my attention from the answers I seek to that which you wish to allude to.

CHARLIE: *(laughs)* I travel to India and live amongst the soldiers. They reform the people and guide them to civilization. Where they had been hungry, they were fed. Where there had been chaos, the soldiers supplied order. Where they had been savages, the white man brought government and structure. Though conquered, who are the people of that place? Are they of that place or are they of their reformers?

When I was a child, I lived at my nursemaid's breast. While my parents were well read, she had been ignorant, yet charged with my upbringing. Then am I of nobility of my parents or the poverty of my nursemaid? If I am of one or the other, can one not move fluidly from one house to the other? As so I have done in my life. None of which is false, but merely an adaptation to that of my surroundings.

HANK: Is this a form of survival? This fluid adaptation of adjusting to your surroundings? What would happen if you remained you in every situation? Would you parish?

CHARLIE: I would no longer be Ernest.

HANK: You would be dishonest, or no longer yourself?

CHARLIE: Yes.

HANK: As it is Mr. Henderson...

CHARLIE: I am still Ernest. It is quite questionable of a man with an education such as yours to continuously forget simple things as a man's name, as I doubt it is of pointed insult that you do such.

HANK: Despite your claims, sir, I fear that little can be done of your condition. You claim to be earnest, all the while failing to take responsibility for yourself in the face of facts, there is nothing more I can do for you.

CHARLIE: More? All you've done is made a feeble attempt to prove me as not Ernest. I hardly see how that has improved my illness at all.

HANK: And what physical illness do you believe you have?

CHARLIE: I no longer appear as myself. I look as if a stranger every passing day. I fear that I am becoming that which I am pretending to be all along. Am I my father's son? Am I my wife's husband? Or am I the persona I provide to my critics. Am I a doctor or a patient? I believe the latter is true.

HANK: Again, this is an illness of the mind. Now I bid you a do.

CHARLIE: Is not the mind of the body? *(CHARLIE stands in unison with the man on the other side of the wall. In mirrored motions, both men approach the threshold, adjusting their coats and examining their face in front of each other as if both faced a mirror, looking at each other as if looking at themselves. Both men gather their hats and exit stage opposite each other but in step).*

The Community

Characters

>JANNETTE, a 40 something year old woman

>MICHAEL, JANNETTE's husband

>NANCY, JANNETTE and MICHAEL's daughter around 20 years old

Setting

>JANNETTE's bedroom. Present time.

At rise, JANNETTE is swiftly looking for something in the room.

Michael stands in the corner by the door watching her.

MICHAEL: You're never going to find it.

JANNETTE: Then why don't you be so kind as to tell me where you put it.

MICHAEL: If you don't know where it is, then there is no way for me to tell you where I put it. Even if I could tell you, I'm not sure I would.

JANNETTE: *(Stops searching and looks at MICHAEL unimpressed)* Well now, aren't you diplomatic? There are only so many places in this room you could have hid it. I will find it eventually. You just sit back and annoy the shit out of me like always.

MICHAEL: What do you need the gun for anyway?

JANNETTE: I have to do it. If I don't stop her now, you heard what the oracle said would happen.

(JANNETTE continues searching for the gun)

MICHAEL: You can't mean Nancy. Jannette, you can't kill your own daughter. OUR daughter. Have you lost your mind?

JANNETTE: *(stops searching and throws her hands in the air)* What choice do we have? You heard the oracle. If we don't do something to stop her it would mean complete destruction. The wall will fall, the enemy will get in and all will be lost. I hate that our daughter is the link to complete anarchy, but it is our duty to do what we can to stop it; to preserve this life for generations more.

MICHAEL: Duty. Not a duty to this family. How many times do you have to make that mistake before you realize that killing her is not the only answer. Don't you love our daughter?

JANNETTE: I love her more than anything I am. I love her more than I can contain in my body. But if we are not able to see passed these things to the bigger picture, it won't matter how much love we have if we have lost everything. *(sits down on the edge of the bed with her head down)*

MICHAEL: Not everything the oracle says comes to fruition. You know this or else you would not try to alter the future she saw. Surely there is another way.

JANNETTE: There is no other way that will definitively work. We can't even risk the slightest chance.

MICHAEL: There is time. We can think this out. We will think of every possibility. What if we send her away to another village?

JANNETTE: How would that stop her from falling in love, Michael? It sure didn't stop you. You're her father, you should be an expert in such things.

MICHAEL: I only know what you know, Jan. You can speculate how I think all you want. It is not going to get us any closer to solving this. We could make her undesirable. Give her a nasty scar or something so no one would want her.

JANNETTE: *(laughs quietly)* Undesirable? That girl could have the face of a hound and still be able to charm the boots off any boy in this village. She's my child you know. We could arrange her marriage to one of the counsel families.

MICHAEL: *(smiles)* See! There you go! I mean, she will never agree to that either, but I've got you thinking!

JANNETTE: Have you ever thought, what would happen if that oracle was just full of shit? I know I'm not supposed to say these things out loud, but who are you going to tell? If I said that to anyone else I'd be standing before the counsel for treason. I really don't think they'd kill their own children, but

I also guess they pay enough money, the oracle would never require it. Soldiers don't have hearts. We just do as we are told. What if this whole system is horse shit?

MICHAEL: Then I kind of wish you would have come up this sooner. But all joking aside, what if it is? What if all this oppression is simply to control everyone? Nancy is young, beautiful, and smarter than most of them on the counsel. Is it possible that they feel threatened by her and want her gone? Scared that their sons will fall in love with her and corrupt them like those biddies at the nunnery?

JANNETTE: Then show me where the gun is and I'll use it on the counsel.

MICHAEL: What happened to your duty, Hun?

JANNETTE: I hate when you call me that. I'm a soldier, not a pet.

MICHAEL: Is it because you can't forgive yourself?

JANNETTE: It isn't about forgiveness, Michael. It's about doing what's best for the greater good.

MICHAEL: At whose expense? Not theirs. Why do you keep going along with their schemes? How can't you see how corrupt the counsel is?

JANNETTE: *(stands up and begins yelling)* If there wasn't a system all would be lost! I did what I had to do to protect what we have. I have come to terms that I do not own anything in this life, including you. If my family must be sacrificed for civilization to survive, then that is the price I will pay. You knew what you had going into this. Maybe you should have left me when you had the chance!

MICHAEL: You don't remember do you?

(JANNETTE looks at him confused)

MICHAEL: You don't remember why I was banished from my home and forced to your village to become a soldier? I told you why. Is that something you blocked out?

(a tear falls down JANNETTES cheek)

MICHAEL: Because I wouldn't kill a child in my own village. They killed the child anyway, and then trained me to ensure I would follow orders. I still would never do it. But I never imagined that you would.

JANNETTE: *(sobbing)* They told me to. They told me I had to do it. Just like I have to now. We have to maintain the order. It's our duty.

MICHAEL: It's YOUR duty, Jan. I'm just here to make you feel better about it.

JANNETTE: But I don't. I tolerate you because I can't bear to let you go. But I don't feel better. I feel empty and alone. Why won't you just understand that I had to and let me be ok with that.

MICHAEL: *(angry)* Because as long as you can't forgive yourself, I will never let you forget how it feels. I keep coming back so you can keep telling yourself that I never left. But I did, Jannette, and I am never coming back. When you can be honest with yourself, try being honest with our daughter. I deserve that don't I? You know she will hate you for what you've done. More than you hate yourself!

(JANNETTE walks quickly toward MICHAEL and he fluidly moves out of the way. She pulls down a picture off the wall to reveal the gun hidden behind it and turns toward MICHAEL)

JANNETTE: She will never know.

(JANNETTE points the gun at MICHAEL and fires. MICHAEL doesn't flinch. He stands silently for two seconds and leaves the scene)

(NANCY swings bedroom door open)

NANCY: Mom! Are you alright?! What are you doing? Who were you talking to?

JANNETTE: *(Without looking from the space where MICHAEL stood, she slowly lowers the gun)* I was talking to your father.

NANCY: Mom, Dad was executed for treason five years ago.

(JANNETTE looks at her daughter and raises the gun again. Lights go down)

NANCY: MOM! NO!

(Gunshot)

END OF PLAY.

Sneak Peak of Apparent Power: Book 1 of the DiaZem Trilogy

Now Available

Chapter One

The electricity flew from her fingers to the shower door handle. Valerie Russell yanked her hand back. The shock had not hurt, but the burst of light caught her off guard. She reached again, slowly. This time, nothing happened, and she stepped into the shower. The water flowing over her face was satisfying in that it woke her senses far better than her alarm. Startled out of her thoughts by her husband clearing his throat, she took a breath to tell him what had just happened when he cut her off.

"Who the hell are you?" Scott stood frozen, staring at her.

"Last time I checked, I was your wife." She wiped the layer of droplets to clear her view and waited for him to respond.

His lips parted to speak, but he remained silent, brows creased, and head tilted.

"What is it?" She stopped the shower. Studying his expression, Valerie pushed the door open and yanked a towel from the wall. The question he posed to her was odd, but his demeanor made her heart race. Something was wrong. She had seen him speechless twice in the seven years she had known him: once when their son was born and again when the boy had broken his arm. Scott had frozen in shock. Her mouth went dry, and the grip of fear tightened her chest.

Scott pivoted when she rushed by him, mouth still groping to form words. Valerie flew down the hall to her son's room and slapped the switch on the wall. The two-year-old scrunched his nose and threw an arm over his eyes. Relieved, she guided the switch to the off position and pulled the door until the opening was an inch wide. Valerie exhaled. Pausing to take a few long breaths, she fought to slow her heart and walked back to her bathroom.

"Stop being weird," Valerie said, shivering. The towel just covered her front, and the cold drops from her dark sienna hair annoyed her. She shoved him. "You scared me."

"Have you looked at yourself today?" Scott asked.

Tight-lipped, she raised a brow, daring him to joke about her body. Scott pulled the towel from her loose grip. The heavy terry cloth fell into a heap on the floor. He reached out to touch her bare skin, but she pushed his hand away.

"I love you, Scott, but we don't have time for this." Valerie kissed his cheek and laid a playful slap on the same spot.

He grabbed her wrist as she tried to walk away.

"I said we don't have time."

The reflection in the mirror caused her to choke on the last word. The figure moved with her as she stepped closer. She rubbed the remaining beads of dampness from her face and studied her reflection again. Her eyes narrowed, and she leaned in further. A swarm of butterflies released in her stomach. The hair stood up on her arms. Her mouth dry and uncomfortable. The thirty-five-year-old working mom stared at the image of her twenty-year-old self. All signs of age erased.

She turned back to Scott, eyeing him as if he might have something to do with what was happening. Trembling, she faced the mirror again, expecting to see the stress-worn image of the woman she saw while brushing her teeth just moments before. Tracing her hands down her body, she compared the figure in the mirror to herself. Her skin was taut and smooth. Breasts lifted and firm. Her stretch marks from pregnancy were faded. The pocket of flesh created by her C-section scar was undetectable, replaced by flat, long muscle. She raked her hands through her damp hair. The thick tresses were like dark silk through her fingers and flowed over her shoulders. Her search for gray was unproductive.

"You look amazing," Scott whispered behind her, wrapping his arms around her slender frame.

"This isn't real, Scott. Am I sick? What is this? The static. . ." She shook trying to articulate. "There was this huge static when I grabbed the shower door. I swear, like a whole twelve-inch bolt of lightning." Ignoring his gentle caress on her bare skin, she squinted into the mirror, wrinkled her nose, and pursed her lips together before resting her face. Her skin remained supple, her features soft.

"Now I kind of wish I had called off work today." Scott bent down to kiss her neck.

"Get off of me! Hon, something is wrong. This—" she turned to face him and waved her hands over her body, "—just does not happen. Fairy godmothers don't pop in and give you your twenty-year-old boobs back. And abs? I have never had abs. Pizza belongs here," she said, poking a finger into her abdomen.

"Well, how do you feel? Do you feel sick or strange?" He laughed. "Did you hit a Gypsy woman with your car recently? Should I be wary of pie?"

"Really?" Valerie rolled her eyes. "I can't go to work like this." She whipped back around to the mirror.

"Well, you need to decide because it's already five and I have to go. But that," he motioned at her body, mimicking her, "is mine when I get back."

"What am I supposed to do?" Her stomach flipped, knowing he had to leave. She wanted someone outside of her head to tell her what to do. She wanted him to stay and help her sort this out. Even if he could stay, Scott was far too distracted to be of any help.

"You can call off if you want, but you'd have to come up with a damn good reason. The staffing office was already desperate, or they wouldn't have asked you to cover a shift an hour and a half away." Scott sighed, "Think of it like this: no one there knows you any different. You'll be fine. Then you're off for a week and can figure things out." Scott kissed her head and grabbed a handful of her backside, pulling her closer to him.

"Okay. I know," Valerie said grabbing the thick straps of his overalls and pulling herself up to stand on his steel toes. "Be safe. When do you think you'll be home?"

"We're taking a train to Wyoming. I'll bring one back tomorrow around the same time. We're hauling coal. The trip is pretty routine as long as none of my engines lose power. But if you don't stop this, I'm never leaving." He kissed her mouth slow and soft. "I'll call you when I get to the hotel." He left Valerie standing naked in their bathroom, fighting the angry swarm in her belly.

Valerie continued the debate of whether or not to go to work. She would be the only nurse on shift at a stand-alone emergency room. She laughed to herself, pacing, and thinking of the least bizarre way to explain why she could not go to work. No amount of rationalization would calm the tremors in her hands and her growing queasiness. She forced herself to rush through her morning routine in hopes the more normal she acted, the more normal she would feel.

She cinched her navy-blue scrub pants as far as the drawstring would allow. Her waist had shrunk more than just a few inches, and the uniform looked like another person could fit in them with her. Frustrated, she flung the closet door open. Taking care not to trip over the shoes on the floor, she tiptoed to the back corner shelf where a pile of her old, pre-pregnancy scrubs sat. Though they also required cinching, they fit better and looked less like a circus tent over her now slender figure.

A loud chime came from a panel on the wall, making Valerie cry out. One hand white-knuckled the counter while the other clutched her chest. The nanny had let herself in, and the front door had triggered the chime. Valerie closed her eyes and inhaled for a measured three seconds before releasing. Knowing she would eventually have to face someone, her nanny, Gia, would at least be more objective than her husband had been.

Before meeting Gia on the main floor, Valerie peeked in on Caleb one more time. The shift was her third twelve-hour day in a row, and she missed him. It was difficult for her to fight the urge to hug and kiss her sleeping son, but she knew waking him would be a mistake. If he were to wake up, he would be in the worst mood for Gia. With Scott driving freight trains out of town and back, she often navigated parenting with only the help of her nanny. Knowing she would soon have an entire week home with her son helped her to walk away and let him sleep.

"Good morning," Valerie chimed, overcompensating for her internal struggle.

Gia sat her heavy school bag down next to the front door and removed her shoes but stayed by the door. Valerie kept on her path from the stairs to the kitchen, terrified Gia would notice her appearance, or worse, not notice at all.

In the kitchen, Valerie poured a cup of coffee. Breathing deeply, she hoped it would ease her tension, but found little solace in the steaming cup. She looked down at the dark beverage. Heart pounding, hands shaking, she took another breath. Her anxiety got the best of her.

"Am I crazy," Valerie asked, "or do I look significantly different to you?"

"No. Did you color your hair?" Gia shifted her weight, rubbed her forearms and elbows, and took a short glance in Valerie's direction.

"Are you serious? I lost like twenty pounds overnight, and you ask me if I colored my hair? Look at this," Valerie said, raising her voice. She pulled the drawstring free of a slip knot and stretched the waistband three inches away from her torso.

"Oh, well, now you point it out, they do look loose," Gia answered, chewing her lip and refusing to validate Valerie's concern.

"I'm losing my mind. I am having a mental break down at thirty-five." Valerie pulled her hands through her hair, gripping handfuls at the root. "Gia, please, just look at my face."

Gia took a step back as Valerie approached. The nanny made no expression, nor did she examine Valerie's face. She looked at her dead in the eye.

"I'm sorry," Valerie said backing off. "I am a wreck. And I'm late. I didn't mean to scare you."

She glanced at the clock on the stove and gathered her lunch, throwing random food items into her bag. "Scott took a train to Wyoming this morning. He won't be back today. I'm working at the ER down south, so I'm out of town, too. The number is on the fridge if you need it. I won't be home until maybe nine tonight if there is no traffic. Caleb can stay up and wait for me if he wants."

"South? Like the Springs? The drive is almost two hours away, more in traffic."

"If you can't stay late, I can call off. The facility might have to close, and I will probably get written up, but with the day I am having so far, I have no problem staying home."

Gia continued to chew her lip. After a few seconds, she smiled and clapped her hands together. The sound made Valerie jump. The changed expression on the nanny's face also startled her.

"No, it's fine." Gia's voice was cheerful but exaggerated. "I will take care of everything here. No need to rush home. Take your time. Caleb and I will be fine." She pulled her thick curly hair back and tied it with a band. It made a big light brown pom-pom on the back of her head.

The coffee in Valerie's mug rippled but did not quite splash from the tremors in her hands. She opened her mouth to protest but was cut off.

"You can go. It's fine," Gia encouraged, but even with her attempt at a natural tone, Valerie could still sense the shakiness in her voice.

Valerie hated passive aggression, secrets, or unresolved disputes. "Alright, what's going on? You are obviously not yourself. I mean, neither am I, but I've owned up to my psychosis. What's bothering you?"

"Umm, school? I have a new teacher. A new class, I mean. I'm not thinking about a guy or anything. I mean, the teacher is a guy, but it's not a boyfriend thing," Gia scrambled for an acceptable answer but fell flat in her attempt to lie.

"I'll call you once I get settled at work if we aren't busy." Valerie did not have time to pry any further if Gia remained adamant about her undisclosed uneasiness.

The two stood in silence for a moment, and then Caleb let out a whine from his room.

"Alright," Valerie said, "you two have a good day. Text me if you need anything at all."

Gia's shoulders dropped as she sighed with relief. Valerie curled the weight of her bag onto her shoulder and left the kitchen. When she reached for the door leading to the garage, a visible arc of electricity shot from her hand to the knob, a three-inch space, accompanied by a loud pop. Valerie shook her hand as if it had hurt, more out of habit. She let out a frustrated breath, grabbed the handle again, and was able to enter the garage without incident.

Within minutes, Valerie merged onto the highway to bypass the city of Denver. The sun had not yet given a hint of light to the sky, but the dark drive provided an isolated environment to mull over the events of the morning. When she passed the airport, two cars exited, and she was alone except for a few oncoming headlights. She replayed the conversation with Gia. The way the young woman had acted bothered her. Gia always seemed honest and straightforward. Maybe she planned on quitting . . . But Valerie needed Gia. With the unpredictability of Scott's schedule, Valerie would have to stay home with Caleb. She did not trust anyone else with him.

Or maybe Gia did notice. With increased traffic and oncoming headlights, Valerie caught glimpses of herself in the rearview mirror. Her transformation was still evident. Gia must have been lying. Valerie just could not figure out how any of this was possible. In her thirteen years of nursing, she had never heard of anything like what she was experiencing.

"You're fine. No one knows you. Just get through the day and get home. You can sort everything out then," Valerie whispered out loud to herself, repeating the speech in variations to not allow herself to turn the car around. Scott was right. After her shift, she had the week off to make better sense of the situation.

On the south end of Colorado Springs, Cheyenne Mountain

loomed over the city. From the highway, she could see the dozens of antennas at the summit marking the NORAD command center, a protected government facility operating the world GPS system. To her, the towers were just part of the scenery, like the barbed wire topped chain-link fence surrounding the base. Traffic flowed with uniformed men and women going to and from their posts. Between growing up with her father in the military, her brother becoming a police officer in the Army and her marrying Scott while he still served, she felt right at home.

She had not told her family she had taken the shift near them. Her and her father, Mike Burton, had a strained but tolerable relationship. Her older brother, Kevin, was still in the military and they never had much in common. For a split second, she considered asking her father, a known conspiracy theorist, about her condition. He would demand a logical explanation and assure her nothing good would come of her transformation. She decided to leave her father out of the equation until she had a better idea of what was happening.

Still deep in thought, her classical music cut off. The gages on her dashboard fell flat. The vehicle coasted down a hill toward a stop light just south of her destination. Valerie threw her coffee mug down to the ground and gripped the steering wheel, pumping the brakes to no avail. She employed every muscle in her upper body to maintain course without power steering. She slapped the triangular button for her hazard lights and pushed her horn, but nothing responded.

Most vehicles continued as usual, but two cars coming from the opposite direction were losing momentum up the hill. She watched one get rear-ended as she sped closer to the bottom. Her shakiness from the morning intensified. Her vision narrowed and a cold sweat broke out on her forehead. She knew what was to follow. What a hell of a time to pass out. Valerie fought against the feeling. With her last attempt at controlling the car, she pulled the emergency brake and pointed the car at a distant mile marker.

Thank God Caleb is home.

Did you enjoy The Brightest Firefly by Dacia M Arnold?

Please leave her a review on Amazon, Goodreads or Facebook!

Dacia will even hang out with your book club!!
Interested in interacting with author Dacia M Arnold?
Reach out to her at
https://daciamarnold.com/contact-us
or email her at dacia@daciamarnold.com

Acknowledgments

Dacia would like to thank a few people who contributed in some way to the production of this collection: Stephanie Flores, Amy Delcambre, Shaula Brown, Cherie Munyon, Tom Clise, Donna Munro, Tim Pike, Darci Kunard, Kayla Fender, Kristen Kruse, Jacqui Riley.

Briana Lucero for wrangling my kids while I worked.

To My AMAZING Patrons: Jack, Kyria, Laci, and Stephanie.

To my ever-patient husband, Greg, who gives me the world and keeps me grounded. Thank you for sharing this life with me.

My sweet, perfect and adorable children. I love you two so very much.

To everyone who has touched my life in anyway. THANK YOU!

About the Author

Dacia M Arnold is an award-winning American novelist, freelance writer, mother, and ten-year Army Veteran. She has a pipe dream to one day narrate an episode of Drunk History, but until then her friends must settle for unsolicited rehearsals. She lives in Denver with her husband, two kids, and beagles Watson and Molly.

CPSIA information can be obtained
at www.ICGtesting.com
Printed in the USA
FFHW020750180519
52537648-57976FF